Death Is Sweet Revenge

I0546302

Death Is Sweet Revenge

ROGER BAKER

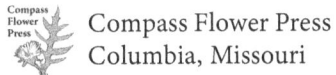

Compass Flower Press
Columbia, Missouri

Cover art by the author

Compass Flower Press
Columbia, Missouri
compassflowerpress.com

Library of Congress Control Number: 2022923692

ISBN: 978-1-951960-46-9 Trade Paperback

ISBN: 978-1-951960-47-6 Ebook

Dedicated to:

My wife Janice and all friends and relatives
who have given support to my attempts at serious writing.
A special thanks to Mrs. Elaine Presley
and Mrs. Joyce Webb.
Thank you, Joyce, for really believing.

Chapter 1

About fourteen months had passed since the death and downfall of the dirty bureaucrat, Oscar Crawford—an assistant director of U.S. Homeland Security—and the destruction of the South American Noah Crime Cartel. Phil Phelps had been in Europe going through treatments for his advanced aging syndrome. The rest of the residents and personnel of Knight's Gate did not know Phil Phelps as a person, they knew only his undercover persona of Philo Peabody, an old man with a severe antisocial disposition. But in reality, Phil, a forty-something government agent, was almost totally responsible for Director Crawford's downfall and the destruction of the Noah Cartel. I was involved in the whole adventure because Crawford and the Noah Cartel were responsible for my father's death in a murder-for-hire and money-laundering plot.

Phil and I never really arrived at any recognizable relationship during his time impersonating an old man while he trailed the Cartel's murderous scheme. But before his departure from Knight's Gate we reached an understanding of a possible relationship in the future. Over the last fourteen months I had received secret, personal correspondence from Phil, and I had replied in kind. Philo's old gentlemen friends here at Knight's Gate also received notes and letters appearing to show Philo's progress from his treatments for his antisocial disorder. His writing became more mature in content, and there was less radical wording in his style. Fourteen months ago Phil, as Philo, was a resident of Knight's Gate, serving undercover for about two years. The treatment for antisocial behavior was only a cover for his time in France. The reversal of premature aging was the actual reason for his French hospital stay.

1

Phil informed me that his treatment for premature aging had gone very well and he expected to be released from his treatment regimen in a very short time. He assured me I would not recognize him when we next met, but he felt I would be pleasantly surprised. I had been dreaming of the moment of our reintroduction and hoping that our relationship would blossom. At the age of thirty-five, I would enjoy the attention of a desirable man after being divorced for a few years.

But, for the present I would have to wait a while longer and carry on the charade of Philo's hospitalization. And in the vein of one of Phil's undercover axioms, "Continue to play the game!"

Chapter 2

As I continued to wait for Phil's return from France, I was not certain how he would reenter my life. Since his physical appearance had changed, I probably would not recognize him. And, he would have to remain a stranger to his old friends at Knight's Gate. They knew him as Philo, not as a younger man named Phil. They could not be allowed to know who he really was because of his job as an undercover specialist. I also did not know if he would return directly to Galeton (the city in Illinois where the old gentlemen's home of Knight's Gate is located) or go through his agency's office in Chicago. The fake organization he is responsible to, as Philo, is the Peabody Foundation, also located in Chicago. I have not heard from the Peabody Foundation since Phil went to France. Perhaps after the Crawford/Noah Cartel ending, the Peabody Foundation ceased to exist. I believed it existed purely for Phil to have a hiding place as he dismantled the Noah criminal organization.

Besides, as the owner/operator of Knight's Gate Retirement Home for Mature Gentlemen, I had plenty to keep me busy. And as the "adopted" daughter of the four senior board members of Knight's Gate—Ralph Cramp, Sandy Gallman, John Niles, and Leo Smiley—who are also co-owners, I was always on the move.

The five of us had gotten the home running as a highly professional business. We renovated the building to remove some unused facilities and reassigned the space for more needed facilities. A fairly large area at the end of one wing that had been planned as a two-ambulance garage, but was never completed, was turned into extra office space for an expanding staff. The other wing had a similar vacant space that was turned into a female living area for nurses and doctors, with a larger bathroom and shower plus two visitor's quarters. In the past fourteen months we had also expanded to a full

3

complement of twenty residents. Actually there were twenty-one of us living on-site—sixteen old gentlemen, my four old partners, and me.

We expanded the workforce to ten medical attendants, one attendant for each two old gentlemen. We also hired five paramedical trainees (Giggling Girls) to assist the attendants.

The kitchen staff also increased. Miss Jessie Crum is chef with a complement of three other assistant cooks. Miss Jessie's meals are legend at Knight's Gate and for most of the surrounding region.

Also, to approach a more professional business level we hired a licensed physical trainer. Hector Ross was a man in his early thirties, olive-skinned, with the body of Apollo. He kept the young ladies' attention most of the time. But he also kept the old gentlemen in top physical condition.

The last of our new hires would arrive in a short time. He was clearing his last employment and would report in as a medical gerontologist. His job would be to provide for the health and welfare of our residents. We hoped to assure that we would never have to repeat the story of Simon Ott, an old gentleman who died because we all overlooked one of his medical conditions.

For the last year I had been able to take some time off, away from Knight's Gate, so I could expand my medical knowledge by attending various nursing classes at surrounding colleges and universities.

When Phil would finally get back from France and make his reappearance to me, he would have a real challenge as to how to present himself to Cramp, Gallman, Niles, and Smiley. Whatever we decided on, it had to protect his undercover credentials.

Chapter 3

One morning as I settled myself at the computer in the office, I casually picked up the morning mail and thumbed through the various pieces. My eyes fell upon the return address for the Peabody Foundation on a very official-looking envelope. It was addressed to me and was marked personal. Rapidly my mind conceived several thoughts.

Was Phil back in Chicago and wanted me to know, without the others knowing? Was he going to return to Knight's Gate as his new personal self, Phil? Or, was he going to come back to see me for a short visit? Since the cartel fiasco was finished, I had no solid idea as to what the letter might mean. Earlier, I had definitely come to the conclusion that the Peabody Foundation no longer existed. So, as my curiosity rose I quickly opened the letter to satisfy my questioning mind.

"Madame Jordan,

It is with extreme sadness and anguish that I, as spokesperson for the illustrious Peabody Foundation, have been assigned the task of informing you, as a dear friend of the late Philo Peabody, of his untimely death.

As you already know, he has spent the last year and some months in a French asylum being treated for severe antisocial behaviors. Sadly, at the high point of his return from those treatments, after almost total recovery from his maladies, Mr. Peabody was killed when his living quarters were destroyed by an explosion from an apparent gas leak in his apartment.

It was one of his requests, and perhaps his most fervent, that five people were to be notified in the event of his death. Number one, Abigail Jordan, two, three, four, and five, Ralph Cramp, John Niles, Sandy Gallman, and Leo Smiley.

Since all of you appear to reside at the same address, would you please convey this sad message to the others aforementioned?

One other request was also found in his personal effects. If at all possible, at his death, his remains or ashes be interred on the grounds of Knight's Gate Retirement Home for Mature Gentlemen, the only place he regarded as his home and his friends as family.

There are very little remains in our possession, actually a few ashes. If your company sees fit to consider or honor Mr. Peabody's last request, please advise, affirmative or negative.

With deepest regrets,

Wanda Bowls,
Spokesperson for the Peabody Foundation"

As I read the letter, tears came to my eyes, and I found myself crying. Then a soft chuckle escaped my lips. Philo never really existed. He was a cover personality for Phil Phelps, allowing him to do his job in ending a huge crime element. But, Phil was so convincing in his portrayal of Philo Peabody that he was able to worm his way into all who knew him, even me, and I knew the truth of his existence.

Well, I didn't know what I would be burying at Knight's Gate. But, if even the memory of Philo Peabody could be enshrined there, IT WOULD BE DONE! That is, if there was no city ordinance against it.

I quickly decided I would simply check with Leo Smiley. He, being a former lawyer and judge for the great state of Kentucky, would know or could find out. But, one way or the other, Philo, the little shit, would rest at Knight's Gate forever.

Chapter 4

In a few days a special delivery package was dropped off at Knight's Gate, with another "very personal" directive to me.

When I opened the small rectangular box I discovered a highly decorated platinum urn bearing the engraved name Philo Anthony Peabody and the dates 1950–2020. Also engraved within a stamped wreath were the words, "Rest in Peace."

I immediately called the *Galeton Gazette* and filled them in on the plans for a future burial of a past resident of Knight's Gate Retirement Home for Mature Gentlemen. I also explained that the burial would be in the yard of the retirement home. (Leo Smiley had done the research and found we could establish a cemetery on Knight's Gate's grounds, as long as the remains were cremated and in a sealed urn.) Of course, it cost the home a few dollars for the permit. Quite a few dollars in the state of Illinois.

I laid the story on thick, explaining that Philo considered the hallowed grounds of Knight's Gate the only real home he ever had, and his friends at Knight's Gate the only real family that loved him.

I invited the *Gazette* to come to the funeral and learn the story of an old man's sad existence and untimely death. Needless to say the reporter was greatly interested in such a human-interest story. He said that he, or some other reporter, would be present to cover the affair. I also told him a memorial banquet would be served to the residents and guests in honor of our old love, Philo Peabody.

As the plans for the funeral continued, I hired a ground crew to come and prepare a nice flower bed to surround the burial and ordered a gravestone that would be placed above the platinum urn.

In my mind I decided I had become quite the businesswoman. The show we were putting on would give Knight's Gate a lot of publicity and add more cover to Phil's credentials, which caused me to wonder, *Would Phil show up for his own funeral?* That thought brought a little giggle to my lips.

A week and a half later, on a bright Saturday afternoon, the time arrived for the solemn affair. The service was scheduled for twelve noon, with a banquet to follow at one thirty.

About 11:50 a.m. a black Cadillac Escalade with the Peabody Foundation logo painted on the side pulled up to the curb in front of Knight's Gate, and one lone figure in a black suit dismounted the driver's seat. As he approached the burial site, everyone observed he was carrying a beautiful wreath made of live flowers and green foliage. He slowly advanced upon the open grave, which amounted to a round hole in the artificial turf, slightly raised above the level of the ground. Carefully he placed the wreath about six inches from the opening in the turf and bowed his head as his lips silently moved in prayer. Stiffly stepping back from the wreath, he turned and walked back to the Cadillac, reentered the driver's seat, and slowly drove away.

Everyone in attendance began to quietly murmur. Being in charge of the affair, I walked up to the wreath to take a closer look, and then I saw the envelope containing a card. I extracted the small message and read it aloud to the crowd.

"In memory of my only uncle, I bid farewell and God's peace."

It was signed Paul.

A red-hot flash passed through my body as the name Paul registered in my brain. That was the name Crawford and the cartel knew Phil as. Was it Phil who had just made a visit to Knight's Gate? Had Phil just come back to his own funeral? As I tried to think of what the man looked like, I suddenly realized I had paid no attention to what he looked like, I only saw the wreath.

Then another of Phil's axioms surfaced in my mind: "My actions will divert attention from who I am to what I am doing."

As I returned the card to its former spot, down on the corner of the envelope I saw three letters: PTG.

Then in my mind I heard Phil's voice once more, "Play the game!"

As my heart fluttered, I turned my attention back to the program at hand and carried out the burial of Philo's remains without a hitch.

Both the *Gazette* and the local TV station, KGI, were capturing every moment of the affair.

Because Philo had never claimed to be a member of any religious denomination, it was decided a short, simple reading would be done in reference to God's redemptive power, and a recitation of his obituary would be given, what little was known. His obituary consisted of his birth date, his age, and his being a relative of the founder of the Chicago-based Peabody Foundation.

One of our old gentlemen residents was a retired minister, and he agreed to do the reading, the eulogy, and the burial prayer. The service lasted barely ten minutes, and then Cramp and Smiley carried the platinum container to the burial spot. The urn was lowered into the hole in the earth, the wreath was then placed around the hole, and a few moments of silence were observed as the existence of the persona Philo Peabody was relegated to its final resting place.

In the background I could hear weeping and clearing of noses and throats as Philo's old friends bid him farewell, not knowing or suspecting he never really existed. So, in playing the game, I also wiped tears from my eyes as I knelt next to the beautiful wreath and bid a sad farewell.

After a short time to visit and memorialize Philo, the crowd moved into the building, advanced to the dining room, and prepared for the feast Miss Jessie had so lovingly prepared. And once more I observed her as she tearfully lived through her own personal grief. Philo was just one more of the little love affairs she experienced as she fed and took care of our loving old men.

Chapter 5

A few evenings later, I had just returned from a light dinner and made myself comfortable as I continued to think about why Phil's agency was faking Philo's death. I ran everything I could think of through my mind, but nothing made any sense. I wished Phil would make contact so I could at least get some type of explanation.

Well with Philo's or whoever's remains interred in the outer yard, I'm sure it was extremely important the charade was carried out with pomp and circumstance. And it was even reported on the local evening TV news. Feeling very proud of the results of the past few day's events, I decided I would take a day or two off from Knight's Gate and chill out at my duplex and try to contact Phil if I could discover a way.

There was a light knock at my door, and as I opened it, one of the attendants stated there was an emergency in Billy Ashfort's room. The attendant said, "Billy appears to be ill, but I don't recognize the symptoms."

I picked up my cell phone and keys, and we proceeded down the long hall to Billy's room. We entered, and I immediately saw white foam around Billy's lips. I rushed to the bedside and knew at once Billy was in extreme distress. I hit a key on my cell phone and the speed dial instantly connected me with the local hospital and ambulance service. I rapidly explained that I had a gentleman in severe medical distress and we needed help. As I turned back to Billy, I felt he was not breathing as our young attendant attempted to administer life-saving techniques. In just a short time the siren announced the arrival of the medical team, and in a couple more moments the attendant and I were surrounded by white-uniformed emergency technicians. As they went directly to their task, I felt a deep darkness start to creep through my being. I remembered, I had lived these moments when Simon Ott went down. Then the lead technician said something to me, and the only word that registered was "dead."

As I feared, the technicians turned to me and continued. "Ma'am, are you in charge here?"

I answered in the affirmative.

"Ma'am, I will need to call the local law enforcement, as I question if this was a natural death."

I was so stunned I could not answer for a couple of seconds, then I queried, "What happened? He just finished the evening meal a short time ago and he was totally well, I believe. Did he have a stroke or a heart attack?"

"No, ma'am, on his lips there's a strange substance; I believe he ingested poison. An autopsy will be performed and then we will know for sure."

About fifteen minutes later, Detective Bradley Blank arrived from the Galeton police department and gave me a hug. After going through the Noah Cartel nightmare together, the murder of my father, and the killing of his grandfather, he understood what I was feeling.

"Abby, what happened?"

"Brad, I really don't know. Billy was fine when we finished the evening meal. He was able to talk four or five others out of their desserts. Fact is, he even convinced me to give him mine, and he carried it with him to his room. Any time he could corral extra desserts he was in seventh heaven. He was even whistling as he came back here to his room. If he got any poison, I can't imagine how or when."

"Abby, stay strong, we'll figure this all out like we did the last time. I'll let you know what I find out as soon as I know."

As he turned away I heard him on his phone, calling his headquarters for a forensic team.

By that moment all the other residents of Knight's Gate were in the hall trying to see what had happened. Cramp was by my side, and I felt him place his hand on my elbow and give me a little help as I felt my legs weaken and my whole being beginning to sag.

"Brad can take care of this right now. Why don't we hit the kitchen for a cup of coffee?" And with that, he guided me down the hall toward the dining room.

Chapter 6

As Cramp and I silently sipped coffee, I wondered, *What happens now? If Billy was poisoned, how did it happen? Or, the bigger question, why did it happen and who was responsible?*

Cramp must have been thinking along the same lines, or he was reading my mind, as he absently stated, "I thought all of this crap was over when the Cartel was smashed and we realigned the operation of Knight's Gate. If Billy's poisoning was not accidental, then what the hell is happening now?"

In a very short time Detective Blank appeared in the dining room and joined us at the table.

"Abby, we will not know what happened until the autopsy results are released in two or three days. The medical people believe he was given or took poison. I concur with their thoughts, so we will handle this as a murder until we know otherwise. The forensic team is taking the room apart trying to find any evidence of what really happened."

Then Brad's demeanor changed.

"We found a dessert plate and spoon on his bed stand, with a small amount of sugared almond dessert still on it. The team is taking it for testing to see if there is anything in the remains."

Then a chill ran through my body. The only plate of dessert Billy carried back to his room was the one I allowed him to talk me out of. If it was poisoned, that dessert was probably meant for me.

"Brad, the dessert you found in Billy's room was the one he convinced me to give him, off my table. If it was poisoned, the poison was probably meant for me!"

I heard Cramp mumble under his breath, "The damned cartel story all over again, when we thought that crap was all behind us!"

13

Brad took on a concerned look and said, "Abby, don't eat or drink anything on these premises until we get the lab results back."

Then my former plans ran through my mind once more. "I was planning to take a little break from my routine here for a while and stay at my apartment for a day or two, to just rest and relax. Cramp, can you handle the operation for a few days while I hide out at the duplex?"

"Not a problem, Abby. Just make sure you prepare your own food and that it comes out of a sealed can. I know it doesn't sound the most appetizing, but it's the safest until we know what is taking place around here now."

While I packed a few personal articles, Brad stood guard in the hall outside my door and then offered to drive me to the duplex so no one but the three of us would know where I went. I thanked Cramp for his help, and then I slipped out the door with Detective Blank.

In a short time we were at the duplex, and I left Brad's sedan and started for the door.

From behind me I heard Brad say, "Keep your door locked, and I will have a cruiser make regular passes by to assure you're okay. You have my number on your speed dial if you need to use it."

Chapter 7

I had settled into my apartment for a few days to allow my mind to catch up with everything that had happened in the past month. I still wondered why Phil had not tried to make contact. I was having a hard time getting the fake Philo death and the real Billy death out of my constant thoughts. Philo's demise made sense in my mind because Phil could no longer play the part of an old man, now being a much younger man. And, he might be planning to replace Philo at Knight's Gate in some other capacity. With the strange death of Billy Ashfort, perhaps he was already involved in some way.

"Damn, I wish he would let me know what is taking place so I can make some plans for my future."

On the fifth day of exile to my duplex, I received a call on my cell phone from the Peabody Foundation. The voice I talked to sounded a lot like the secretary I had talked to at the government agency Country Freedom.

"Ms. Jordan, the Peabody Foundation is aware of the beautiful service you and Knight's Gate performed in the burial of our family member, Philo Anthony Peabody. The foundation realizes there was a large outlay of money for such a special occasion. The board of directors felt that it is only fitting for the Peabody Foundation to reimburse you or your business for said expenses. Therefore, in a short period of time, probably today, a representative of this foundation will deliver a check for twenty thousand dollars to cover said expenses."

"But ma'am," I said, "the cost of the funeral and service was much less than that amount, so let's discuss the cost. Besides, Philo was one of our own, so we do not feel that reimbursement is necessary."

15

"Madame, the Peabody Foundation would be embarrassed in the financial world if they did not take care of their own. If it is an embarrassment for you or your company to accept payment, use the money to establish a care memorial for Philo Anthony Peabody's grave, so it will be cared for in perpetuity. Our representative will deliver the check in a short time. Thank you, Ms. Jordan, for your assistance in this matter. Goodbye."

As I cut the connection on my cell phone, I became more and more confused. What did Philo's death and burial have to do with anything? I thought, *Phil, this is one hell of a strange game, but what does it have to do with anything? But, I promised to always play the game, so here I am. Bring on the other team and maybe I can at least play defense even though I don't know how the offense works.*

After a short bathroom break, I decided to just chill and read for a while and wait for the next move in this deadly game of chess...or whatever the game was.

Not that day, but about 1 p.m. the following, Cramp called to tell me a messenger delivered a twenty-thousand-dollar check to the office from the Peabody Foundation. The messenger also left a letter explaining it was to cover the expenses for Philo's burial. I then explained that I had received a call the day before from the Peabody Foundation with the same explanation. Cramp laughed a little as he said, "I suppose old Philo was about as wealthy as the rest of us, he just didn't know it."

Chapter 8

About a week had passed, and the autopsy results were still in the lab. I was concerned, so I called Brad Blank, and he said there were some difficulties but he felt the findings were very close to being released. So I was spending my time reading and napping, and had just settled in for another round of time-wasting.

As I read, I felt my eyelids becoming heavy so I closed the book in my lap and allowed the darkness of sleep to carry me away to the world of dreams.

In my mind I heard the clanging of trolley bells as I rode up the hills in San Francisco, even as I knew I had never been there. What a surprise, a vacation on the west coast. I heard myself giggling as I suddenly sat bolt upright and recognized the sound of my little apartment's doorbell.

With a bit of grogginess still controlling my thoughts, I fumbled my way to the door. But, before I attempted to open the door I forced myself to be wide awake. I slid to the window and peeked from behind the drapes and saw a Peabody Foundation vehicle in front of my door.

Before I opened my door I loudly asked, "Who's calling?"

A voice answered, "Someone with a message from Country Freedom and a message from Phil."

"One moment please," I answered, as I brought up Detective Blank's cell number on my phone. And then I held the phone behind me with my finger on the dial button. Next, I opened the door with the safety chain still in place.

As I looked out the crack of the open door, I saw a medium-built man carrying a briefcase. But he kept his face and eyes looking down toward the toes of his shoes.

17

"I'm looking for Abigail Jordan."

Then cold fear took over my whole body as I realized no one knew I was here except Cramp and Blank. I started to slam the door, but a different voice said, "I've waited fourteen months for this moment; please don't lock me out. And I'm sorry Philo had to die."

Tears streamed from my eyes as I rushed to unfasten the safety chain to allow my man to come through the door.

Then I saw his eyes, and a tiny twinkle of Philo looked back at me. It wasn't him, but a part of him was hiding just out of my sight. Phil stepped through the door, and I quickly closed it behind him. Then I remembered to take my finger off the dial button and place the phone on a stand nearby.

We took each other's hands and did the silly little circle walk, like two children, as we simply looked into each other's eyes.

Then a different look appeared in Phil's eyes as he said, "Abby, I won't kiss you right now. We've been apart for a long while and I know how things can change over time. I'll wait until we have time to get reacquainted, in case anything has changed. We really didn't have time to know each other before I left."

Before he could say more, I put my hand over his mouth and asked, "Have you changed since you left?"

He reached up and removed my hand and answered, "Only what I look like, not about you."

I grabbed him in a bear hug and placed the most sincere kiss on him.

"Nothing has changed, I said I'd wait, and here I am."

Then a confused look took over his expression. "Abby, I'm sorry, now I don't know what to do. I've never been this close to any girl or woman before. After high school I went to work in law enforcement, in undercover work, so I didn't have time or opportunity to get involved with women, and now I'm embarrassed, I don't know what to do."

I took a step back and slowly looked at the man in front of me. He was about three inches taller than I, his features were young and soft, his eyes were those of Philo, and his hair was a golden blond.

"Phil Phelps, I'm sorry too, because you are stuck with me unless you bodily throw me out of your life. I've thought about you a lot over the last year or so, and I want what I see. I also understand that your job will take you away at various times, and I can live with that. My job takes me away from my personal life sometimes, and you will have to live with that. We don't even have to marry for me to be your love or your wife, if you want that. And I am not ashamed to teach you how to be around a woman, if you would want that."

Then before I could say more, he kissed me the way I wanted him to, and he did a fantastic job for a man who didn't know how.

Chapter 9

After an hour or two of getting reacquainted, my curiosity finally got the best of me, and I said, "Phil, I think we have finally convinced each other that we should be a couple, but now I must know what has been happening at your end." I quickly explained what had happened to Billy and how the medical team and Detective Blank believed it was murder. And that perhaps I was the intended victim.

Phil suddenly became quiet and reflective. "I got here too late! Yes, I would say you were the intended victim. Luckily or unluckily for Billy, you did not get the poison."

I gasped, "Billy was murdered and I was the actual target?"

"Yes, that is also why Philo's character died. There are some leftover problems from the Noah Cartel case. You remember I told you Crawford, before he died, was out to kill you and Philo because he believed you were the instigators of the actions to bring about his and the cartel's downfall. That information filtered down to his and the cartel's families, and they are out for revenge."

"But I still don't quite understand how the death of a man who didn't really exist and then died makes any sense."

Phil then told me the whole story.

"Abby, I was Philo...so he did exist. The enemies believed he, I, was involved in bringing them down. They wanted revenge on that person, no matter who he really was. They also wanted you dead, and they knew who and where you were. Since Philo went to Europe for treatment, they decided to wait for him to return before they put their plan into action. And they thought a cooling-off period would make it easier. Our man, the one spilling his guts about Crawford, kept us apprised of the planned goings on. When Philo announced his return, they decided to put their plan into action. We didn't know the whole plan, but we went on the offensive. As soon as I got back to Chicago, I got into makeup and became Philo once more. Shortly a stranger began to show up at some of the same places I did. We zeroed in on him and discovered he was casing a way to get to Philo, so we decided to let Philo be the bait.

"First, Philo, since he was almost a whole human being, moved into a building on the Peabody Foundation grounds. Oh yes, my love, the Peabody Foundation is a real place, except it does not work to save worn-out animals, it's a wing of the agency Country Freedom. What the enemy did not know was that there was a secret passage from the building Philo moved into, to the brain center of the agency in the main building. I never stayed in Philo's house; I simply went in the door and out the passage so I could watch the man following me.

"Second, I played Philo to the hilt. You understand, Philo was not as radical after his treatments, but he was still a squirrel. He still said and did things that caused people around him to believe there wasn't much light on in the attic. This caused the man following Philo to become lackadaisical. Philo was leading him, he wasn't following Philo.

"Third, our gutless man divulged that the man I was following was a hired killer. Crawford's and the cartel families did not know who he was, and they paid him in advance, not knowing if he would ever complete the job. The only rule was, Philo was to die. In a way this would have been a funny wrinkle if it had not been so serious as to be a hired killing, because my agency was trying to come up with a way to make Philo disappear. After all, I was now back as Phil Phelps. The killing idiots were going to solve two problems at once. Philo would die and the killer would never be heard of again. Oh yes, my love, I'm sorry, but you have a paid killer buried in Knight's Gate's yard."

After catching his breath, Phil continued. "After all the snares and nets were set, the agency allowed me to be cornered in Philo's little house. The area had been cleared and sealed off so no innocent person could be in the area. The only two allowed into the building were Philo and a little later the killer.

"I was in my pj's and preparing to climb into bed when the assassin made his move. He was good but proved later to not be good enough. He appeared out of nowhere and was beside me almost before I knew he was there. The only thing that saved me was his aftershave. I smelled him just as he moved in close.

"The moment I saw him I went into Philo's persona as I jumped and threw my hand up to feebly defend myself. He sneered and laughed as he grabbed my arm. He was so sure of himself he wasn't even wearing a mask. As I shivered and begged for him not to hurt me, he began to brag. First, he told me how many people he had killed in his career. Second, he told me how he was going to kill me. He was going to suffocate me and then hang me, so it would look like a suicide. I begged him to let me put on my sleeping mask so I wouldn't see him hurt me. When I asked that, he roared with laughter. But he allowed me to get my mask off the nightstand next to the bed, and that was his undoing. A tiny barb was attached to the edge of the mask, and you know the rest."

"The same poison you used on Carlo Santos!"

"Bingo! Then I turned on all the burners to the gas cooking stove, walked out of the little building, waited about thirty minutes, and dialed Philo's phone that was on the bed stand. There was an explosion and fire...case closed. Now, does that clear up what you wanted to know?"

"But wasn't there a DNA test to see if it was Philo's body?"

Then Phil giggled, "Remember, Philo never was. What DNA would they compare it to?"

For a moment I felt as if Phil really enjoyed killing the man. And then, like I did when he killed Santos to save my life at Knight's Gate, I remembered his job was to protect the innocent and bring the criminal to justice. And sometimes someone will die. Thankfully, when Phil's around it is the criminal.

But then I had a sudden question. "But how did you not blow up the main building if gas was in your little house and there was a passage to the main building?"

"Abby, the buildings we occupy were built during the Second World War for military use. They were designed to allow one portion to be sealed away from the other portions, in case of an outside attack. When I went from one building to the next by the secret passage, the passage was always resealed."

Then the conversation took a different turn.

"Abby, did you recognize me in any way when you first saw me?" Phil asked.

"No, but after a few minutes, your eyes reminded me of Philo. But why do you ask?"

"I am going to be your new medical gerontologist. And I want to know if you think any of the old friends will see through the deception and realize I'm the person they knew as Philo."

"Cramp is a pretty shrewd old man, and he might be like me in a way and start to wonder."

"Any suggestions as to how I might get around him?"

"You might try contact lenses with a different eye color. Or, I wonder if some odd-shaped glasses with plain glass might throw him off?"

"If I removed the glasses, then he might still suspect. I'll see an optometrist and get fitted with the contacts. Then I'll let you check me over again."

"Be sure to wear a medical jacket when you are working; that might distract him a little also." Then one more burning question zipped through my mind. "Do you know enough about gerontology to bluff your way through?"

"While I was taking treatments, I was also questioning everything that was done to me because I was very curious about my case and old people in general. I believe I can keep myself in a correct direction and at the same time not cause the old guys any harm." He paused. "Before I leave, could we practice a little more on boy meets girl?"

I grinned and moved in on him quickly and with determination. After a few minutes, he said, "I believe it's time for me to leave and give that lesson a lot of thought."

Before he got out the door, I asked him, "Where are you going to live?"

"The agency has set me up in a rather swank rental apartment becoming a doctor of gerontology. Oh, by the way, here is my phone number if you need to contact me. I already have yours as the agency secured it for me earlier."

Then I remembered one last item that had been on my mind since Philo's interment.

"Were you the one who personally delivered the wreath to Philo's grave?"

"Yes."

"Then you did appear, alive, at your own funeral?"

Then he giggled, and with one last kiss he cautiously slipped out the door.

Chapter 10

In a couple of days there was a knock at my door and a voice said, "The doctor you called is here for your evaluation."

I recognized the doctor's voice and rushed to answer the knock. When I opened the door, there stood a doctor in a white jacket with a name plate that read, Doctor Phil Elliot. It was the same man who had called a few days before, but his face appeared different some way. Then it registered—his eyes were no longer green; they had become almost a black shade of brown. Now they did not twinkle; they had almost a burning effect. Had I not known who he was, I would not have recognized him. He was also wearing what appeared to be bifocal glasses, which distorted his eyes' shape and movement.

"Will this fool ole Ralph?" he asked.

"I believe it will; it almost scared me, before I decided that you were Phil."

"Are you going to welcome me back, or are we going to have to start our reacquaintance all over again?"

"No, I believe I can close my eyes and see the man from a couple of days ago."

With that I grabbed him again and we wasted a few more minutes before we got back to the task at hand.

The first thing we discussed, before I forgot to explain, was about Alma living next door. I told Phil she worked during the day, so she would probably not see him. But, if she did I would have to have some type of story to cover him coming around.

He had already thought that through and explained it to me. "Abby, if we are a thing, we won't be able to hide it for long, so we may as well come out of the closet, so to speak, and just become a couple. There shouldn't be anything wrong with the owner and one of her doctor employees seeing each other. Here's how we will work it—I'll lay low for the next few days, and then after I've worked at Knight's Gate for a week or so, I'll just ask you out on a date and we will simply hit it off with each other. It will be good because we will work and play together and I can be around you to protect you as we try to find out who is the killer at Knight's Gate."

Then my mind jumped back to the present. "How can I go back to Knight's Gate, if I can't eat on the premises?"

"Simple—you will serve yourself from the kitchen, dip your own food from the pots and pans, and eat before you vacate your table or plate. If you drink anything, same plan: fill your own coffee mug or glass of liquid and don't vacate it until you have finished. Besides, I don't think they will try poison again. Too many people will be watching the food and drink."

We joined up on the couch and went back to practicing boy meets girl for a little longer before Phil had to leave. He may have been an older dog, but he sure was learning new tricks at a rapid pace. I thought I might have to get a partner so we could double up on him.

Only joking; he was my old man, and I intended to be his only teacher.

Chapter 11

After Phil left my apartment, I thought over his suggestion as to how I could return to work and decided to make the approach. As if on some type of cue, my phone rang and it was Brad with the autopsy report.

He began his report by telling me Billy had indeed been poisoned and the poison was of a usual type that his lab identified as common ant or roach poison. The only fact they knew for sure was the poison should not have been strong enough to cause the death of a man in reasonably good health. However, the autopsy also revealed Billy had some other problems that indicated the poison could have caused his death. Then he explained that the poison was found in the dessert remains that Billy had conned me out of that evening. As fear shot through my body, I realized the poison was meant for me, but why a simple insect poison? Was it to make me sick as a warning of some kind?

After a few moments the fear subsided and I told Detective Blank I thought I would go back to Knight's Gate. He objected, but I told him of my plan, the one Phil had described to me. After a bit more discussion he finally gave his consent. As a legitimate argument I told him I needed to get back to running my business. And, I used Phil's point that the killer would not try poison again because everyone would be watching.

Then Brad retorted, "Remember, Abby, there is more than one way to skin a cat. And I'm afraid you might be that cat! But, the real question is, who would be out to try to kill you?"

I knew it was the cartel again, after all Phil had told me, but I couldn't let anything slip. Phil was in charge, and I knew he would do everything he could to protect me.

"Brad, I have no idea, but I guess we will just have to wait and see."

Or as my mind played the old tune—we'll just have to play the game.

As I broke the phone connection, I was already gathering the things I would need back at Knight's Gate. In less than an hour I was back at the home, ready to return to my daily routine.

Chapter 12

As soon as I walked in the front door at Knight's Gate everything seemed to move right back to normal. Billy had been taken care of and returned to his family's hometown for burial. Cramp had kept everything moving as if nothing out of the ordinary had occurred. I found Miss Jessie in the kitchen and explained to her how I would be taking my food for the foreseeable future. She seemed to have an odd expression on her face as we talked. So I asked, "Jessie, is there something wrong?"

"Do you want me to quit and leave? My cooking killed Mr. Billy and I supposed I was to blame and I couldn't blame you for thinking that, Ms. Jordan. So if you want me to, I'll leave."

I threw my arms around her and hugged her with all the strength I could muster and whispered in her ear. "Miss Jessie, you would be the last person on earth I could ever suspect of putting poison in any food. I know you love the old guys as much as I do. Someone did poison poor Billy, but I know it wasn't you!"

A smile slowly crept across Miss Jessie's face as she said, "Thank you, Ms. Jordan, for believing in me. Yes, I love them all. They're all like my old granddaddy, and I loved him more than anyone else I can think of."

Then I knew why she felt so bad when we lost Simon, Philo, and now Billy. She was reliving the loss of her beloved grandfather.

As I left the kitchen, Cramp was walking up the hall toward me.

"Abby, have you heard anything about what happened to Billy?"

I immediately knew Brad had not contacted Cramp about the autopsy findings. I supposed he did not want to go over my head with what had happened at our business. So I explained what I had been told.

Then Cramp asked the same question he had asked earlier. "Abby, what the hell is going on around here? This seems to be a replay of the damned cartel nonsense. Are we going to be a business that experiences a murder about every year or so?" Then his expression changed a little, and he very seriously asked, "Abby, is there anything else you know that you are afraid to tell me?"

I lied as I replied, "No, all we can do is try to protect each other and wait, perhaps, for more information on the poison, if there ever is any."

Cramp nodded his head and said, "Okay," as he turned and walked away.

I felt like a low-down bitch as I went back to my chores. But, I knew I could not divulge any of what Phil had told me or I would remove the one advantage we had over the killer—that Phil was who he really was.

Then a warm feeling swept over me as I fully realized who he really was. Phil Phelps was the man I loved and the man I intended to spend the rest of my life loving, either as his wife or as the woman he could always return to. But someday, and soon I hoped, he would become totally mine. But a second but, I will wait until he decides it's the right time for me to teach him about all that. With a tune in my mind I returned to my daily tasks.

Chapter 13

The plan worked smoothly. I sometimes ate in the dining room and sometimes in my own rooms, but I always served myself. I watched all the residents, attendants, and staff but saw nothing that appeared to be another attempt at putting poison in the food. And I knew Miss Jessie was twice as vigilant as I. She was very proud of her cooking skills, and she did not want anyone to think she made a mistake that would make someone sick, or worse, kill them.

However, Cramp still appeared to be a little cautious of me. I knew he was shrewd and very intelligent, so pulling the wool over his eyes would take someone a lot smarter than me. Phil could do it, but I didn't have that kind of guile. I decided I would have to talk to Phil about it and see how we should go about handling that smart old man.

Speaking of Phil, one morning about three or four days after my return to Knight's Gate, a taxi pulled up in front of the home and a well-dressed man stepped out onto the curb. He paid the driver and then surveyed the front of the building. One of our attendants joined him outside the door and escorted him inside. I saw the light-colored hair and the glasses and knew my man had finally arrived to fill his slot in the medical corps of Knight's Gate.

I quickly walked forward and extended my hand as I explained my assumption that he was Dr. Elliot and welcomed him to Knight's Gate. He took my hand and carried out the charade as we became acquainted—boss to employee.

Cramp also came forward and introduced himself as part of the Knight's Gate family and also welcomed him to the staff, as I sank into the background and allowed the rest of the staff to become acquainted. As I retreated I told Phil I would be in my office if he had any questions and that Miss Jessie would be serving her usual fine lunch fare in a very short time and that he shouldn't miss it. He thanked me and said even the people in his new apartment house knew of Miss Jessie's reputation and he was looking forward to lunch.

As Phil turned away to continue to talk to Cramp and the rest, he handed me an envelope, explaining it was his complete resume and work history. I thanked him and moved off to my office. On the corner of the envelope were the letters PTG.

Once seated at my computer console I opened the envelope. Along with the resume and work history there was another sheet.

"I will meet you at the Walmart parking lot at 9 p.m. We need to work out all we plan to do to fool the opposition. Since we do not know who or exactly what, we have to be extra careful. By the way as soon as you read this, be sure to totally destroy. I will go back to the old way of communicating, using TP or Kleenex stuffed into the mail slot in your apartment door. Soon we'll devise a way for you to leave messages for me. Love you. *John.*"

By signing that way, even if the killer found the note, no one would know who or what, from our end either. But I immediately tore the note into small pieces and flushed it all down the stool.

Miss Jessie's lunch was superb, as usual, and I noticed Phil did not waste a crumb. I'm sure he remembered her meals from the past. And with a little luck I might get to be a little more dessert around 9 p.m.

Chapter 14

I was on pins and needles all the rest of the day. At 9 p.m., I would get to be with Phil again. I was beginning to feel like a silly schoolgirl with her first boyfriend. But, in a way Phil was my new boyfriend, after a few years being single. And, we were going to try to set up a plan to flush out the killer or killers at Knight's Gate. The only bad part was that Cramp was having thoughts about some of my actions, and I didn't know what to say or do.

At 9 p.m. I was in my car on the edge of the Walmart parking lot. I had taken a long way there as I twisted and turned to throw off anyone who might be following me. I was sure, as thorough as Phil was in his investigations, he would know my car even without ever having seen it. At about 9:05, a rough-looking creature walked out of the shadows and started toward my car.

However, before much fear had boiled up into my mind, the creature removed his cap and I saw his pale hair. I knew it was Phil. I pressed the unlock button for the doors, and he climbed into the passenger seat next to me.

"Are we clear?" he asked.

"I've seen no one," I answered.

"Let's drive as we talk; it's harder for anyone to get close enough to hear, and we will not cause anyone to be suspicious of two people sitting in a car in Walmart's parking lot."

As I pulled out of the lot he removed part of his costume and became Dr. Phil Elliot. Before he was able to begin our discussion of the problems, I added my problem to the list. I told him about the comment Cramp had made, which seemed to indicate a degree of suspicion.

"For now, Abby, just try to smooth over anything he asks or says with whatever comes to mind at the time. If he's already suspicious, more bull will not change what he believes a whole lot, and it allows us to continue the plan we put in place. Perhaps down the road we can take him into our confidence and tell him the real story. What about the other three, do they seem suspicious?"

"No, they are so happy with the lifestyle and living conditions at Knight's Gate they are not looking at anything that will change how they feel. They are totally content with the status quo."

"Good. They will probably not be bothered by the killer, and at the same time they won't get in our way. Now, what do we need to do?" he asked.

"I don't know. I was hoping you would have a fantastic idea."

"Okay, I have one. We talked about becoming a couple pretty quick, so now is the time to put that part of the plan into action. And the sooner we do it the less chance we will slip up and someone else will see through us or get overly suspicious. And, besides that, I can't wait to put my hands on you every chance I get."

With that I pulled to the curb and parked in the small residential neighborhood I was driving through and made my own move on him once again. This time he was prepared. He still didn't make the big move, but I knew there was plenty of time for that. So, I just enjoyed the necking for as long as he was willing. At 1 a.m. I decided it was time to call it a day and get home to prepare for the coming morning. If I appeared out of sorts, someone would wonder why.

I dropped Phil near his apartment and continued on to Knight's Gate. When I was safely locked in my rooms I dialed Phil to let him know I was safely at home. We said good night, broke the connection, and I headed for my bed. I could hit the bathtub in the morning. Besides, I could still smell the scent of him, and I wanted to continue to enjoy that until I was sound asleep.

So I whispered, to no one, "Good night, my love."

Chapter 15

There came a slight disruption to life at the Gate with the delivery of a letter from a law firm in Demont, Missouri. It stated the family of Billy Ashfort was bringing a wrongful death lawsuit against Knight's Gate because of Billy's poisoning. I immediately became extremely concerned, as a lawsuit of that type would bring a lot of bad press to the home.

Leo read the charges and said to not be overly concerned, as a murder investigation was ongoing at the time and the home was not really responsible for the murder. But, if or when the killer was apprehended, some responsibility might fall on Knight's Gate. However, if it should, our umbrella liability insurance plan would cover any claim up to five million dollars. So, he said he would continue to follow the claim and inform the family we would cover any liability that might be judged against the Gate, at the proper time. Knowing how well-informed Leo was, I felt much better knowing the family would receive any and all settlement due.

After that, for the next few days, I continued to listen and watch everything around me. Nothing appeared in front of me that caused me any more distress. So I began to prepare for Phil to put his plan into action.

Later my thoughts returned to my being the target for more of someone's hatred. Then I remembered a little blurb I had read somewhere: "Revenge is a meal much sweeter and best served when it has been allowed to become ice-cold!"

I thought, since they believed they had gotten Philo, then tried to get me with poison and failed, perhaps they had decided to let me stew and worry for a while before they would try again, making the revenge much sweeter. So I decided to try to continue as if nothing had happened and hoped to survive the next attempt on my life. I really felt better knowing Phil was nearby.

And Phil was wasting no time; within a week he let it be known that I was on his radar screen. Almost overnight everyone knew he intended to try to win my affection. Little did they know he would not have to work too hard as I was ready for the assault.

First, he had Miss Jessie prepare a special dinner, which he paid for, to honor all the other staff members. When the dinner was served, he made it his business to join me at my table to dine with me. He brought a special bottle of wine and drank a special toast to me before he shared the bottle with the rest of the staff and me. I was sure he drank first to prove the bottle was not poisoned. During the meal he also let it be known that he hoped to have more time to enjoy dining with me. Cramp and the rest of the older diners did not know how to take the activities. The young ladies thought it was very thoughtful and cute. I thought perhaps it was a little sudden, but if it worked I was all for it.

By the time the meal was over, I was on Phil's arm being escorted from the building to a waiting limousine, going to one of the finer restaurants in Galeton for a special dessert. Most of the residents and staff clapped and cheered as we left the outer yard. But I noticed Cramp had a serious look on his face as we exited the front door.

As we rode into downtown Galeton, Phil stated, "I believe from now on we will start to appear as a couple."

I kissed him as I agreed. But I still wasn't sure exactly how Cramp viewed the past hour or so and what he might do because of it.

Chapter 16

The next morning, at almost the moment I found my seat in front of the computer console, Cramp walked into the office and closed the door.

"Abby, do you remember a few days ago when I asked you if there was anything I should be aware of and you danced away from the question?"

Suddenly my mouth went dry and a queasy feeling settled in my stomach as I tried to find something to say. I remembered Phil saying to try to smooth it over if I could. "Yes, Ralph, but I don't know of anything I haven't told you."

"But damn it, Abby, you did tell me, back over a year ago."

"What? What did I tell you that far back?"

"You hired Elliot because he's an old boyfriend. I'm not unhappy about that, I'm unhappy because you didn't trust me enough to tell me."

"Ralph, I still don't understand."

"When we were going through all the crap with the Noah Cartel, you mentioned you received a call from Phil. And, I asked you who Phil was and you said an old boyfriend. And now you've hired him and were ashamed to tell me. I nor the other three even knew he was being hired."

I knew my back was against the wall, and I couldn't think of any way to pass it over without totally losing the friendship and trust of one of the old men I dearly loved. So all I could do was fill in a little and hope it would suffice.

"Ralph, as you know, we probably have a killer under this roof. I'm working with the law, trying to discover who it might be. I have been advised that I am probably the intended victim, and I did not want to draw any of you others into danger. So, Phil agreed to help

39

me keep watch and assure that the rest of you are always safe. Please bear with me and keep my secret. All I want is the best for everyone and to catch the killing bastard before he gets me or someone else."

With his head down, Cramp answered, "I know I sounded like a jealous old bastard, but I thought you didn't feel you needed me anymore, and after I had started considering you as my daughter. You're the only one I felt I could really trust and count on. Then this started, and I thought you were pushing me out because you didn't need me. I never thought about you putting your life on the line to protect us. I'm sorry I misread everything and didn't see the whole picture. Abby, please forgive me and I'll try to stay out of the way."

"Ralph, there is nothing to forgive. You want me safe the same as I want you. But I need you. You and the other three are my ears and eyes all over the home. Don't duck out on me, just don't be surprised or alarmed at anything I might do. Just remember, if it doesn't seem right, watch it closely and be ready for action."

"Abby, do you want me to have Sandy turn the room buzzers back on and pass the word that they might be needed? And would your friend Phil want to move into Philo's old room since there's a buzzer already installed? I'm sure Sandy could also explain the operation to him."

"Ralph, let me talk it over with Phil, and I'll tell you what we decide. But please don't tell anyone that Phil is helping me. I don't want him in any danger either; that's why I didn't tell you about him before."

"You can count on me. And now that I know the other game you're playing, if you and Phil appearing to be a pair makes the job easier, I'll really lay it on that I think you make a beautiful couple. Well hell, maybe you will make a beautiful couple—for real."

And with that Cramp strutted out of the room with his head in the air, and I knew he was a true friend through thick and thin.

Chapter 17

Later in the day, by hook and crook, I was able to secure a few minutes with Phil under the guise of discussing one of the older men's foot problems. We went into his office and closed the door. Then we talked aloud and at the same time wrote notes as to the real reason I was there. We did the writing in case someone had bugged our rooms. Phil felt we could never be too careful.

I told him about being waylaid by Cramp and having to admit we were a pair from way back and that he had agreed to help me, undercover, to solve the killing. I also told Phil that Cramp believed our hanky-panky was a put-on so we could work together. And then I told Phil about the thought of reactivating the buzzers and asked if he wanted to move into his old room to be closer to any possible trouble.

Phil was pretty much satisfied with the plan. And he told me to tell Cramp to have Gallman reinstate the buzzers, and he would stay off and on in Philo's old room. In that way he could be close to his patients on a more regular basis. And as far as he and I playing at hanky-panky, Phil thought that was a real hoot. And to prove we could play the game we practiced for about five minutes before I left the office.

The very next day Phil brought personal supplies and extra clothes and put them in Philo's old room as he prepared to spend more time on-site caring for the old men and their problems. Cramp carried out his part as he had Gallman reactivate the buzzers and secretly brief Phil on how the whole thing worked. Phil thought that was another hoot as he already knew all about the buzzer set up.

41

From that time on I rested a lot easier as I felt we would now have a fighting chance if the killer attempted another move. The only thing missing was Philo fluttering in and out as he played his game. But Phil was accepted as one of the group, and since the boy/girl game continued between us, he was believed to be just one of the guys.

Shortly, Phil developed insomnia. *Made up, of course.* Another way of being around the home at any time, day or night. After a few nights, no one thought it strange that he might be walking around anywhere on the grounds at any time of night. He would be seen in his white fuzzy slippers and his bright red-and-black checkered robe. But I knew for a fact that under the robe and slippers he was wearing a ninja costume, and that he had all the training and skills of a ninja warrior. With him within an arm's reach, no simple killer would have a chance of survival in a man-to-man contest. Once more, Knight's Gate had, on-site, the one person who could level the playing field against the remains of Crawford's evil band and the Noah Cartel. Then a thrill ran through my body as it struck me...and he was all mine.

Chapter 18

Shortly thereafter the official report arrived from Brad Blank that the FBI's lab had finally determined what killed Billy. It was a common sugar-based poison for ants and roaches. Anyone could purchase it over the counter to combat household ants and roaches. The product name was "Sweet-num." Probably most households in the city had some on their home care shelf.

Phil and I decided to take time and think that over. And Phil said he would have Country Freedom dig into that latest information.

Phil and my boy and girl thing, by that time, was finally pretty well out in the open, so us being together was no longer a suspicious activity. If we had our heads together no one thought much about it. Cramp still believed it was put on and he was the only one, so far, with any inside information.

Phil was the first one to approach the murder with the actual statement that all the people in the building, save perhaps he and I, were suspects. That statement was like a lightning bolt.

"No, Phil," I said, "not the old guys, they came here to die, not kill someone else!"

Phil answered, "Abby, I hope you're right, but in my business, even a newborn is a suspect if it can move its hands."

"Phil, it had to be one of the workers. They're the ones who handle the food and put it on the tables. It almost has to be a server. Miss Jessie is like a tigress about her food; no one would be able to poison food in her kitchen!"

"Remember, Miss Jessie is also a suspect!"

"No! Damn it, she's not! She loves all the old men and me. She would never hurt us!" I almost screamed.

"Abby, just be careful and watchful of everyone. I don't want to find you dead because you didn't stay on guard."

As tears rolled down my face I whispered, "I know you're right, but suspecting Miss Jessie or Cramp or any of my friends is like suspecting you."

"Abby, just remember how you questioned me about who I have killed. Anyone can do it if the motive is strong enough. And right now we think we know the motive, but are we sure?"

As we returned to our jobs and chores, I had to think deeply about what Phil had just said. And then I said a small prayer. "God, please don't let the killer be one of the people I love so much."

As I wiped the tears from my eyes, one of the attendants walked up to me and said, "Old Dan is having one of his episodes; perhaps you might want to personally check on him and decide what we should do to make him more comfortable. He doesn't want to go to the hospital again. He said if he was going to die, he wanted it to happen here."

Dan Herdon was an older gentleman with severe lung problems. His breathing was assisted by the constant use of oxygen. Sometimes he would commence coughing and continue for several minutes at a time. Many times when the coughing stopped it would appear that he had simply passed away. But in a few moments, miraculously his breathing would start again, and he would rally back to the land of the living.

I called Phil and told him I needed his help in Dan's room. In moments, Phil was by my side as we entered Dan's room. Another attendant was leaning over him readjusting his oxygen tubes as Phil and I came up along the side of his bed. Dan's eyes were watery and his fists were clenched, but his raspy breathing appeared to have returned to its usual pace. He looked up at Phil and me and whispered, "Made it one more time, in spite of the bastards!"

I didn't know what he was trying to say, but I was so happy he was still with us and had the strength to give somebody hell.

When I got back to the office, I looked up Dan's records and found he was ninety-seven years old. I had to assume he was the oldest resident we had. Made me wonder how many times he had beat the bastards in the past. I knew he also loved dessert, so I made a note to tell Miss Jessie to double his portion the next meal he was able to tolerate.

But then my wiser self came to the surface, and I wondered, *Does Miss Jessie have any Sweet-num in her kitchen cleanup and care supplies?*

I decided I would not ask, I would simply play the game and ask if she had anything to combat ants that had appeared in my living quarters. I decided the first time I had the opportunity, without seeming to be snooping, I would ask the simple question.

Chapter 19

Almost immediately after he arrived at Knight's Gate, Phil gathered all the information on our residents and staff and forwarded it to Country Freedom to be analyzed by its staff.

One evening as we were continuing to become more and more reacquainted in his room, Phil stated that he had received the return information about our residents and staff. We decided to spend the rest of the evening reviewing the reports.

The four old friends and the original staff had nothing new in their folders. I had expected that but was very happy to know that others believed they were who they said they were.

Some of the younger personnel were tagged for common law indiscretions, minor drug use, liquor violations, and other very minor childish infractions. One young lady had even been caught standing on the second-floor balcony of a hotel room, totally unclothed, singing, "Take me out to a ball game." And a young man standing below was hollering, "I've got the balls if you have time for a game!"

Most of the rest of the new residents and staff appeared to be clear of any questions or suspicions.

Remaining were four with questions about some simple matters that on the surface did not seem to amount to anything at all, but the agency had flagged them just the same.

Phil took two and I took two and we began to read and reflect on what was being said.

One of the young male attendants had crossed the southern U.S. border more than ten times in the last two and a half years. But since starting work at Knight's Gate, he had made no more trips.

One of the older young ladies, a registered nurse by profession, stated her maiden name was Crawford. Maybe it meant nothing, but it was questionable because Oscar Crawford was one of the bad ones from before. Her married name was Rose Mary Smith. And as everyone knows, Smith is a very common alias name.

Two of the old gentleman residents had a question or two, but they did not ring any loud bells.

Samson Mann had a prison record from many years before, for embezzlement. He had served a ten-year sentence and then was paroled. But it had been thirty years in the past. Then he had worked for another twenty-five years at an honest job and retired with honors.

Then my eyes popped wide open when I saw the next name. Dan Herdon's records had a flag about his former place of residence. Until he moved into Knight's Gate about a year earlier, he had lived in his family home on the Texas–Mexico border. The question was, and no answer was found by Country Freedom, why did he move this far north to live in a retirement home? I could think of many reasons, but if the agency had a question, I felt we needed to be alert.

Phil was bothered with the young nurse having the name Crawford. He felt that we needed to do more research and determine if she was kin to Oscar. We decided to play a few games and attempt to draw out more information by simply talking about things connected to the facts we had to see if anyone volunteered more information. I told him I would visit with Dan and try to draw him out. And Phil said he would work on the nurse as she was around most of the time when he was checking on the old men. We also decided both of us would talk to the young male attendant with the border travel record.

For a while we returned to our original evening activities and then decided to get our necessary work activities completed to be prepared for the next day's work. After a quick parting kiss, I left Phil's room and proceeded back to my apartment. Cramp saw me exit Phil's room and flashed a huge grin as he passed on down the hall.

Chapter 20

Robert Kobb was the young attendant with the Mexico travel record, so I casually approached him in one of our break room conversations about me desiring to see the world. Of course he followed right along and said he had been out of the country a few times, but not very far when talking about the world. I jiggled the bait a little and said, "Where have you been? Tell me about it."

"Ms. Jordan, I've only been across the border into Mexico a few times, and that was when I was dating Marianna. We would go down to visit her parents about once a month, in Monterrey. When I moved up here to take the job at Knight's Gate, I broke up with her.

"I'm sorry!" I said.

"It's okay. Her parents didn't like me anyway; they wanted her to marry an older man who owned a big hacienda with lots of horses." Then he lowered his head a little and continued, "I told them I thought that was a lot of horse crap, and they asked me to leave. Marianna stopped seeing me after that." Then he raised his head and grinned. "You know the attendant assistant Peggy Duff? She and I are a thing now and I believe I'm much better off. She's even said she likes me, a lot, and I know her parents like me as much or more. I think she's a keeper."

We both finished our coffee at about the same time and headed back to work. I had to believe he was in the clear and also a keeper.

The next time I saw Phil, I passed on the new information, and he said we could mark Robert off our list. At least for the near future. I didn't say so, but I figured for the rest of time.

I knew Phil would be working on Rose Mary Smith, but I decided I would try a quick check on a direct route to the information. I sat down in front of my computer and searched for Oscar Crawford's obituary. It was simple to find because of his former status in government and because of the blowup in the Office of Homeland Security. When I located his obituary, it said he had two daughters: Mattie Lyn Crawford and Rose Mary Smith. Then I started to wonder! Why didn't Country Freedom, in their report, just plainly say she was the daughter of Oscar Crawford? Did they screw up on their research or was there something I wasn't getting? I immediately decided to cover that ground with Phil. We needed all the information if we intended to protect ourselves from further fallout.

While I was waiting for my next few minutes alone with Phil I decided I would just bluntly question Dan as to why his family sent him here. I could bluff my way because his place of residence was listed on the forms filled out for him to be admitted to Knight's Gate. It was no big hush-hush piece of information that was found in some deep hole.

Then I noticed it was time for lunch, so I put my thoughts on the back burner and made my way to the dining room.

Miss Jessie, as usual, had prepared more of a dinner than a lunch, and the residents were enjoying their food to the utmost. After getting my food from the kitchen, I joined them in the enjoyment. Phil was evidently busy and did not make it to the dining room for lunch. After finishing my lunch I went back to the work at hand and completed the day.

Chapter 21

That evening after dinner when Phil was off duty, I went to his room to discuss Rose Mary Crawford. I was a little disturbed because I felt Country Freedom had dropped the ball by not doing deeper research into the name Crawford. Especially after I was able to find the facts so easily in Oscar's obituary.

The moment I mentioned the facts to Phil, he became quiet and did not speak for a few moments. Then he volunteered, "Abby, I have known for a while that she is Oscar's oldest daughter. I didn't say anything to you because I was afraid it might upset you. After having to face that SOB in your rooms and believing he might kill you, I felt you might not be able to control your emotions in front of his daughter. So, I decided to keep quiet until I had a chance to ask her a few questions as to why she is here."

I started to make a retort but decided he was telling the truth, so I just replied, "Do you think she's the killer? Do you think she will tell you anything that might be of value?"

"If she's innocent, I don't want to destroy her for no reason."

Then I realized he could kill without remorse, but he was compassionate enough to be fair in fulfilling his duties. Then I knew another reason I loved him.

Once more, I continued, "Are you going to try to be coy in your attempt to get her to talk, or are you going to just ask straight out if she is here simply to be a nurse? It doesn't seem like a coincidence that she would come here to work."

After a few moments of thought, Phil finally replied. "I think I'll just be me and play the game when we are working together and see what happens."

Then I told him I had been planning to just ask Dan Herdon head-on why he ended up in an Illinois old-age home.

51

Phil said, "An old man will either tell you the facts or tell you it's none of your damned business."

"But at least you believe I will get an answer."

"I sure do."

After that we had a little wine, some crackers and cheese, and then we decided to practice a little more of boy meets girl.

Later as I had a moment before bed to give it some thought, I believed we had come to some valid conclusions and sealed our conclusions with some solid activities. As I climbed into bed and settled for the night, I felt safe and contented.

Chapter 22

A few days had passed and Dan had regained most of his former strength, so I decided it was time to tell Miss Jessie to double his dessert for the next meal. And then I felt I had the chance to ask about the Sweet-num. "Miss Jessie, do you have any kind of pest-control products? I have seen a few ants around the plants in my rooms and thought you might keep something on hand to stop any that appear in your kitchen."

"Yes Ms. Jordan, I keep some of the best and safest products on the market. Fact is I have two small containers of Sweet-num in my storage room right now. I'll get you one to take care of your problem."

I casually followed her into the storage area as she went to get the product. When she reached the shelf, she paused for a moment and stepped back to look at more of the shelves. Then she reached out and picked up a small paper tube-shaped container and turned to hand it to me. I immediately saw Sweet-num on the container with the following statement, "Sweet as sugar and deadly as an anteater!"

"That's strange," she said. "I'm sure I had two containers the last time I looked at this shelf. That was about three weeks ago."

I thanked her, turned, and then walked out of the storage room and headed for my rooms. I hoped what I was thinking was untrue, but Miss Jessie had the poison and knew where it was kept. "Please, God, don't let it be Miss Jessie!" I couldn't believe the killer could be Miss Jessie, but now she was more than just a suspect, she had moved into the position of the prime suspect. I had to talk to Phil as quickly as I could.

When I found him, Phil was working with one of the old men in an attempt to loosen the muscles in one arm that had been broken several years earlier. Phil was working with him to loosen and strengthen the muscles so the old gentleman could accomplish more activities with the affected hand.

Seeing he was busy, I gave him a little signal that I needed him as soon as he was free to talk. Then I proceeded to the office to pay some bills that were due at the moment. After a period of time Phil appeared in the doorway and motioned for me to join him as he walked down the hall. I supposed he was headed for the coffee pot and a few minutes of break time. I caught up with him just as he finished filling his cup. After a moment to fill my own I joined him at a table away from the main gathering area.

"Hey love, what's so important that you came looking for me in the middle of the day? I'd love to get involved, but it might look improper at this time of day?"

Then he saw that my demeanor was not the brightest, and he restated the question. "What has happened that has you in a down mood?"

"Miss Jessie keeps Sweet-num on hand all the time. She gave me a container after I told her I had some ants in my apartment. She said she had two containers about three weeks ago, but now one is missing. Phil, she just can't be the killer; I won't believe she would do such a thing!"

As he reached across the table and held my hand, he repeated his earlier statement. "Ab', you may be right, but anyone under certain circumstances is capable of almost any act, no matter how heinous." As I nodded, he continued, "All we can do is continue to watch and stay safe, and perhaps a mistake will be made and we can learn the truth."

Phil arose from his seat and turned to leave the dining room. "Well, break time is over and I have more work to do."

I nodded once more and got up to return to my chores of paying bills.

Chapter 23

As the day wore on I finally decided it was my job to face Miss Jessie and push the point that the poison Billy ingested probably came from her storage room. I thought perhaps she might make some statement that would entrap her if she was the one who put the ant poison in the dessert.

After I finished my bill-paying chores I made my way to the kitchen and found Miss Jessie involved in preparing the evening meal. But I immediately saw that she was not accomplishing her usual level of progress this close to the dinner hour. And, as I came closer to her I saw huge tears in her eyes. When she became aware that I was next to her, she pulled her apron up over her face, and I heard and saw massive sobs rack her body.

"Ms. Jordan! I can't hide the truth no more! I know I probably caused Mr. Billy's death!"

Before I could stop myself I blurted, "Jessie Crum, are you saying you put poison in my dessert and Billy ate it instead of me?"

As more sobs escaped her being, Miss Jessie wailed, "Oh no, Ms. Jordan, I could never put poison in the food I prepare—God would strike me dead and I would go straight to Hell!"

"Then what are you saying?" I demanded.

"Ms. Jordan, I thought when that Noah bunch was killed I was finally free, but they must be back and I'm caught right back in the middle of the whole mess again."

"What do you mean you're caught in the middle again? Were you involved in something before this...this poisoning?"

"I'm sorry! I'm so sorry! I only did it to protect my baby! I was afraid they would harm or kill my baby Boz!"

"Boz who?"

"My baby boy, Bozworth Crum. My son! Oh, Ms. Jordan, I never meant for any of this to happen, but I didn't have no choice. They would have hurt or killed him in prison."

Suddenly I realized that there was more to Miss Jessie's story than just the ant poison, so I paused and allowed my reasoning to catch up with my racing thoughts. As I put my arm around her I gently said, "Miss Jessie, tell me the whole story, and I'll try to help you in any way I can. You've been my friend, and I want to help you if I can."

Dropping her apron from her face and taking a few deep breaths, Miss Jessie began to tell me her story. "Ms. Jordan, I have a twenty-eight-year-old son, Bozworth Crum. Who his father is has nothing to do with any of this. Boz came to me when I was sixteen years old. My old granny said my life would be tough, so she decided to teach me to cook in the old southern way. That's what and who I am today. Boz was young, fast, and reckless. I couldn't control him, and he became a dude of the streets. Before anyone could stop him, he was involved in crime and eventually went to prison in Chicago. Then I got a break, some man said he could help me if I would help him. When he told me what I had to do and how much he would pay me, I couldn't say no. He got me the cooking job here and paid me a wage besides the pay here. All I had to do was tell him when a new man came into Knight's Gate that appeared to have a lot of money. He told me that the people he worked for could skim a little of the man's money while he lived here. I didn't think it would hurt a rich man to lose a little of his money, so I agreed to do what they asked. Oh, Ms. Jordan, your daddy was the first one I tattled on. Oh, God forgive me, I never believed they would kill him. When he died I believed that he really did break out and died of exposure. But...when the second old man, Mr. Sal, died in almost the same manner, I knew it wasn't a natural death that got either one of them. They were murdered. Then you appeared, and in a short time I realized you were digging for the truth. But I didn't tell the man, I just kept quiet and allowed you to do your thing. About that time that Latino, Carlo, told me if I said anything to anyone about what was happening they would harm Boz. But, when everything was moving in the right direction, I gave you the picture with the note inside. I'm sorry, I gave you a lie and lied about it. I wrote the note on the back of the receipt saying that Crawford was connected to Noah. It was the only way I could think of to end the whole dirty mess. And it did! But, Ms. Jordan, I didn't lie about your father. He did say you were the only woman he ever loved."

Suddenly I became aware that another person was in the kitchen with Miss Jessie and me. As I turned toward the door I saw that Phil had quietly stepped inside the door and had probably been listening to what Miss Jessie had said. Not knowing what would happen next, I motioned for him to come to where I was standing. I supposed after seeing me with a befuddled look on my face he stepped in and took over the conversation.

"Miss Jessie, I don't think you're in as much trouble as you think you are. You did scratch some laws, but I don't believe you were involved in any of the deaths that have happened here. But we do need your help to find out what happened to Billy. He was poisoned, and it appears the poison came from your storage room. Do you know if the cartel has any other people working here at Knight's Gate that may be trying to harm Abby?"

"Mr. Phil, when I said I flew to Mr. Ott's funeral I lied again. I was ordered to meet one of the cartel men in El Paso, Texas, to discuss my job with them. All the discussion was...was a threat against Boz and me if I told anyone anything. But, Mr. Phil, I can't be quiet any longer. But, yes, at the meeting I was told the cartel was placing someone on the inside here to be sure I didn't tell anyone anything about the business. So, probably there is someone here, now, who was working for the cartel before it was destroyed."

"Do you have any idea who it might be?"

"That damned Latino grinned at me and said, 'Bitch, he's old as the hills and has been in this business since it began fifty years ago. So don't try anything cute!' Do you suppose he was talking about one of our old men who is here now?"

Phil did a slight double take and then I saw...visualized thoughts churning in his mind. "I'll do some checking," he said.

Suddenly I remembered the dinner hour was rapidly approaching and some of the food still needed to be prepared. Lightheartedly I said, "Miss Jessie, I'll call one of the other girls, and we'll both help you get the rest of dinner ready for the table."

With a tearstained smile Miss Jessie replied, "Ms. Jordan, I'm so sorry, but I would appreciate the help." With that she turned and began to concentrate on the final food preparations.

I phoned one of the girls still on duty and asked her to come to the kitchen to help with the rest of the food preparation. She agreed and was with Miss Jessie and me in a few moments. As I made the call I saw Phil leave the kitchen and proceed down the hall toward the office. I knew he would be involved in the new information for hours and maybe days to come. I was confident that he and his organization would research every person at Knight's Gate until he could find the plant, if there was one. I also knew that later, after hours, we would meet to discuss the latest break and perhaps play our own game for a little while.

Chapter 24

Phil and I talked later and he told me he felt it best to contact Detective Blank to determine the best course for Miss Jessie to follow after her admission to some guilt in the Noah Cartel's activities.

Later that evening he talked to our good friend Blank, and then the next morning he related to me that at first Brad thought it best to just take her into custody for her own and others' protection if she was really more than a pawn in the whole Noah affair. Phil, considering how I felt about Miss Jessie, proposed putting her under house arrest in her own home, so that if she was later determined not to be criminally involved, she would have no repercussions to face. Brad said it sounded good, but he had no officers to spare to ensure that Miss Crum remained in her home at all times. Phil said he had a friend who was trained in criminology and would do it for him and me as a favor. He did not tell Brad that in reality the friend was actually an agent of Country Freedom who would make sure nothing happened to affect the further Noah Cartel criminal investigation. After a slight consideration Brad agreed to that scenario.

After Phil explained the whole plan to me, together we went to the kitchen and explained the entire situation to Miss Jessie. She was upset because she felt she was letting the old men down by not being on the job cooking for them. Then I explained she had trained a couple of the young kitchen assistants plus myself, and we would be able to fill in to prepare the meals until she returned or other decisions were made. After a period of tears and much thought Miss Jessie decided that our plan was the best action for her and for the old men she loved. With no further discussion she collected her personal items and drove away from Knight's Gate. As Miss Jessie was leaving the parking lot I saw a car down the street fall in behind her. I pointed it out to Phil as I fearfully cried, "She's being followed, Phil, do something."

In a low voice he answered, "Another of our agents is being sure she goes straight home." Then a short time later Phil's *friend* arrived to set up the surveillance of Miss Jessie's house arrest. Phil also suggested, if it was still possible, a tap of Miss Jessie's phone might be a good idea. The agent replied he would do whatever was necessary to get it done.

With that chore taken care of it was time to return to the job at hand and attempt to find the true killer of Billy Ashfort.

Chapter 25

Phil and I met later and discussed the latest break. Phil said if there was a plant and he was, as the cartel agent said, "As old as the hills and involved with Noah since its inception," he would have to be one of the older men we housed. Phil vowed he would research every one of the older men until he found the plant or proved there was really no one else.

And secondly, we took time to play our own little game. It had entered my mind that one day it would move from just game playing to a higher level of two-member lovemaking. But I didn't believe Phil was mature enough yet in the boy and girl game for me to attempt to get him into the bedroom. However, I felt it was going to happen sooner rather than later.

The following morning as I started my usual work day in the office, one of the young interns stopped at my desk and asked what he should do with Billy's meager belongings. Brad Blank and his crew as well as Phil, on the sly, had completed their investigations and now the room needed to be cleared and cleaned for the next resident to move in.

"Just put everything in a box and bring it to me, and I'll attempt to get it to his next of kin. Or if there is no one, I'll inventory it and then we'll store or destroy it."

"Ms. Jordan, it will be a pretty small box, because there isn't much."

As the intern turned to leave I answered, "That's okay, we'll still handle it that way as it's the humane thing to do."

A short time later as I continued to do the mundane chores I so dearly hated, the intern returned with a shoe box of small articles that represented the only valuable property that Billy Ashfort probably ever owned. The intern placed the box on my desk, turned around, and walked toward the door. Then he mused, perhaps to himself, "That Billy had things hidden all over that room. I found a little plastic figurine in the finger of an old worn-out glove on the floor in his closet. There was also a little cardboard container rolled up in a crease of the window curtain. But, I guess strangest of all, he had a fake one-hundred-dollar bill taped to the back of a picture on the wall." I heard him but paid little attention as he disappeared down the hall.

A few minutes later, with a small tear or two in my eyes, using one finger I rummaged through the objects in the box. I saw a worn comb, a tattered New Testament, and some small mementos from fairs or carnivals. Then my fingers felt something that was familiar in a strange fearsome sort of way. My fingers closed around a small paper tube-shaped container. I almost jerked my hand back in fear. I had just handled a container like that a short time before. The Sweet-num ant poison container was exactly the same size, shape, and weight.

As my hand began to shake I raised the small container up to eye level and surveyed the object with extreme interest. The container was a twin to the Sweet-num cylinder. It had the same sprinkling top, but the product label was different. The label on Billy's cylinder was for "Sweetin-It." And the ad said, "Sweeter than sugar!" I noticed the label had been cleverly taped around the tube. And then I noticed something else—the tube was sticky to the touch. As if someone had wet fingers as they handled the tube and the substance inside melted and was smeared over the outer surface. Then tears flooded my eyes and I began to bawl loudly as I remembered Billy always licked his fingers after he had eaten some dessert that was really sweet and that he really enjoyed. Billy had handled the poison and had licked his fingers as he handled it. "Oh God no," I bawled as I realized Billy probably poisoned himself! But then the next question raced through my mind. Where did Billy get the container or who gave it to him, and why?

Jumping up from my desk, I actually ran down the halls of Knight's Gate screaming for Phil as my whole body began to shake. Cramp caught me first and demanded to know what was wrong. As I turned to answer him Phil threw his arms around me and began to also shake as he tried to stop my trembling, while at the same time he quietly asked, "Hon' what's wrong?"

Clinging tightly to him I bawled, "Billy was poisoned!"

"Yes, Babe, we all know that," he replied.

"No! No! No! He poisoned himself!"

Shaking me a little to calm me, he demanded, "What are you talking about?"

Then as I slowly returned to a calmer state I explained what I had found. Taking the container from my hand, Phil slowly and meticulously studied the small tube.

"Ab', I believe you're right. Someone made this up and probably gave it to Billy to sweeten his desserts. And if they knew Billy they also knew he would use it on other foods, but why?"

Then I broke into his train of thought and flatly stated, "Billy had no money; he had nothing. Why would anyone harm such a helpless soul?"

As pure hate flashed from his eyes and the words grated between his teeth, Phil growled almost like a wild animal as he replied, "I really don't know, but if we catch the creature I personally will be sure he or she pays dearly for such a crime."

Catching himself stating his hatred out loud caused Phil to bite his lip as he drew in a deep breath. Then as calmly as the part he was playing, in his most professional medical voice, he stated, "Now we need to get this to Detective Blank and let his lab get all the information this little piece of evidence will give us." With the cylinder held carefully in his hand he headed back to his office to call Brad Blank.

Chapter 26

Because it was for Knight's Gate, Brad Blank moved our needs to the front of his lab's work, and we received the results within hours instead of days.

Early the next morning Detective Blank was at my desk with the results of the lab work done on the second poison container. First, the report stated that fingerprints from four different individuals appeared on the container. One was listed as belonging to Abigail Jordan. The second was listed as belonging to Phil Elliot. The first two were very fresh and clear. That made sense as we handled the tube last. The third was listed as the prints of Billy Ashfort. Those prints were all over the tube and were rough and smudged. Also saliva was detected in the prints. And the last print, and only one was found, was almost non-existent. And that print belonged to Jessie Crum. Since she placed the container on the shelf, that was explainable also. No other prints were found.

The second part of the lab report explained the make-up of the contents of the container. The major part of the substance was sugar mixed with a simple ant and roach poison. But after further testing it was discovered that a third substance was also present in the mix. Almost unheard-of in the United States, a poison was found that is used in the jungles of Central America. This poison is an oil from the backs of specific tree frogs that ancient headhunters used. It is used today by modern hunters to treat the tips of their blow-gun darts to kill wild game. The ant and roach poison would not have killed Billy, but the added poison did kill him.

The information did not clear Miss Jessie. But, at the same time, it did not absolutely convict her either. I continued to vote in my mind that she was not guilty.

Phil was not so easily convinced. But the frog poison caused him to step back a little as it was something Miss Jessie would have had difficulty gaining access to. But with a connection to Central America, it would appear that some part of the Noah Cartel was still involved.

To escape from the dark mood that had settled into Knight's Gate after Billy's death, Phil and I decided to take the night off and just go someplace and chill out. So I told Cramp I was leaving for a few hours and that he was in charge. He joked and said, "Nothing serious I hope." I slapped him on the shoulder as I walked out of the office.

Phil suggested we go to his apartment, pull down the shades, keep the lights low, and order in something grand to eat. I agreed and off we went. The mood in his apartment lifted as Phil's demeanor changed almost 180 degrees. He became lighthearted and played the part of a perfect host. The lights were low, the talk was quiet and serious, and the food he ordered almost competed with Miss Jessie's.

Then it happened. Before I was fully aware of what we were doing, we had both undressed and changed into some very expensive sleepwear Phil had purchased as a simple joke. Finding ourselves dressed in the expensive sleepwear, we began to play boy and girl games in bed. When I fully realized what was actually happening, the sleepwear was all over the floor and we were in each other's arms. So much for believing Phil would have to be taught all the finer points of getting it on.

Later I had to stifle myself from laughing aloud as I thought of what Cramp would say if he knew what had just taken place. But tough, he'd just have to live with it...if he ever figures it out.

After that very short pause in the action, I settled back and continued to participate in the game we had initiated. It was an old game to me, but I felt as if I had never played it nearly as happily and as pleasurably as I was playing it with Phil Phelps, alias Dr. Phil Elliot.

Much later I asked him where he learned that new trick. He grinned and said, "I got all the major information off the net from a seventh grade 'Personal Living' textbook used in Illinois public schools."

66

Chapter 27

After such an enjoyable evening...and night, I had very little desire to move away from my new love and love nest. But the clock said, "work time," so I supposed I needed to be back on the job. Phil left much earlier to make it appear his insomnia caused him to get to work in lieu of sleep. He left a note for me saying to join him whenever and how to lock up the apartment.

After a leisurely tub bath and a cooling down period I got dressed and took a taxi back to Knight's Gate. I slipped in quietly and changed clothes so I would not appear in the same garb I had on yesterday. Then it was to the office and back to the daily grind.

As I seated myself at my desk my mind finally kicked back into gear and I remembered I was going to grill Dan Herdon a little as to why he came from Texas to live in our home in Illinois. And I feared, as Phil had suggested, the old man might tell me it was none of my business. Or he might explain it to me in stronger words I wouldn't like to repeat. But, my other sweet old men and my care facility were still in danger, and I intended to protect both if I could. So I decided to take the bull by the horns and just make a simple frontal assault.

I found Dan in a wheelchair in the tiny enclosed garden where the sun shone brightly and warm, with sweet-smelling flowers all around. He looked a bit better than a few days before but still appeared very, very weak. So I decided to play my part with feelings about his condition. "How are you feeling this morning, Dan?"

I saw a slight movement of one arm as he attempted to straighten himself up in the chair. With a hollow sound from his lips, the words came weakly but sincere. "Miss Abby, I don't believe my time here will be much longer. I'm glad you found me as I need to tell you some things before I go. I'm not the man I wish I really was. I came here under false pretenses. I didn't come here because I was old; I came here to do a job of which I'm so ashamed."

After a few long moments of heavy breathing Dan continued. "I was placed here to gather information for a horrible organization. When we started the company it was a simple con game. The Noah Cartel would simply steal a few dollars by playing confidence games. But the power at the top changed, and it became a kill-for-profit venture. I tried to get out, but I was too old and too afraid. The bastards placed me here to inform on everyone and everything. Then I became old enough to die, and here I am."

A hard, dry cough began to form in the old man's chest, and he rocked and racked as the terrible power of death moved ever closer to the surface. After a few minutes he settled back and began to softly whisper more. "When you and Blank destroyed the cartel, I believed I was finally free to die honest. Now I don't know. One of us old guys has been poisoned, but I honestly don't know if it's the old bunch or not. No one has contacted me since the plane crashed, killing the kingpin and the four cartel wheels. Miss Abby, be careful and wise. If it is part of the old bunch, they will want you dead."

With those words Dan closed his eyes and his breathing stopped. I felt fear go all through my body as I heard myself screaming for help. In a flash two of the attendants cleared the door and rushed to my side. Seeing Dan, they both reached his chair at the same time. Then a slight rush cleared Dan's lips as he whispered, "I'm still here; the bastards haven't got me yet. Miss Abby, take care."

The attendants wheeled him in the door and called for Phil and the nurses. I took a few moments to feel myself beginning to breathe once more, and then I followed the group to Dan's room. When I entered the room, Dan was in bed surrounded by our whole medical staff. He had an oxygen mask covering a large portion of his face. His eyes were open and moving around the room. Phil noticed I had arrived and explained it appeared Dan had beaten the bastards of death one more time.

I briefly told Phil a little of what Dan had said in the garden. He replied we would discuss all of what Dan said later when we had more time. At the moment Phil was doing all he could to keep the old gentleman on the living side of the curtain. I respected his dedication, so I left the room and returned to the office and more of the work I was expected to complete. As I seated myself back at my desk, one lingering question crossed my mind. *If Dan was not involved in Billy's death, might Rose Mary Smith be the guilty party?* I supposed Phil and I would discuss that possibility also.

Chapter 28

My day continued as expected. I was able to complete most of the paperwork connected to a few days of Knight's Gate's operation. I was beginning to suspect Cramp was correct when he'd said that we might eventually want to hire out the office operations to a professional firm. By doing that we could enjoy living with and caring for the old gentlemen without the daily headaches of paperwork. I loved the old men, but I hated the paperwork.

At lunch the younger women and I prepared the food. It was not as great as Miss Jessie's, but it was filling and nutritious. No one complained, but I was certain they would have cheered to see Miss Jessie come back through the dining room doors. I knew I missed the yummy meals she prepared.

I made it a daily routine to call and check on her as I felt she had suffered more than necessary. She sounded well but anxious to come back to her beloved old gentlemen. I hoped we could figure this mess out quickly and that she would be permitted to return.

After the dinner hour, Phil and I finally had time to get together to compare notes and make plans. Phil wanted to go to his apartment for more privacy. I thought perhaps there were things on his mind other than old Dan and Rose Mary Smith...there certainly were on mine.

This time I drove to Phil's apartment because I knew I couldn't make a habit of spending a lot of all nighters—someone would suspect our activities, and I didn't need that on my shoulders with all the other problems.

When I arrived at his home, Phil had already developed a plan of action. He felt we should have almost direct contact with Country Freedom as we worked to solve Billy's murder. Earlier he had made contact with the mother ship, and he and his investigation section decided to use the same communication system that had been employed when he destroyed Noah. We would use a tiny transmitter with a range of about a city block to send our information to a receiver being used by one of his fellow operatives stationed in the immediate neighborhood. That way our information would not be picked up by someone hacking into our phone system. It would be the next day before the system would be in operation, but he and I decided we could still compare notes and perhaps a little later participate in other more enjoyable activities.

We decided I should explain old Dan's admission first. So I told Phil everything Dan had said in the garden before we thought we had lost him. Phil replied, "We were very lucky that he did not pick up any of the things we did to stop Noah, and now it appears he has given up being their snitch. But, at the same time we need to continue to hide everything we are doing, so nobody can learn our plans."

Then I asked him, "Have you been able to talk to Rose Mary Smith?"

He said he had been having casual conversations with her, but he still was not sure if she even knew her father was involved with the kill-for-pay plot. When he asked her why she applied to work at Knight's Gate, her answer seemed clear and honest. She said, "I came to Knight's Gate because my father said he had visited and eaten in the home and considered it the best of the best in the nation."

It seemed he had also stated, "Abigail Jordan and her staff run the cleanest and finest old-age care facility in the country!" And she continued, "You understand my father, in his job, had visited many old-age homes, so he would have had a chance to compare many facilities doing the same work. After he died, some of his associates trumped up charges and said he was involved in some kind of confidence scam, but he wasn't that type of man. I applied here because he was impressed with the home and I wanted to be a part of the best there is!"

Then Phil made a statement I found hard to believe. "Ab', I think I believe her, but...we will watch everyone and investigate everyone until we know for certain whom the guilty party is."

Then, before I had time to think, I was overwhelmed by a smooth-talking, warmhearted man and found myself in the bedroom once again. I could put full blame on my host, but I think I was almost as guilty as he, or maybe more guilty. Either way, I was beyond happy having an honest man in my bed who really loved me.

Later when I crawled into my own bed back at Knight's Gate, I began to feel lonely because there were only two bare feet between the sheets. Perhaps I would marry again if everything worked out in such a way that my man would not be afraid to make that big step. I would never want to lose him, but I believed I could stand the loss of him if he were totally mine, if only for a short time.

Chapter 29

I awoke with a start, looked at my clock, and realized I had failed to set the alarm or had simply turned it off in my sleep when it chimed. Either way, I knew the younger ladies would be in the kitchen starting breakfast and waiting for me to appear to supervise the activity. Thankfully breakfast was almost always the same—meat, toast, eggs, coffee, and tea. And all the little oddities, cold cereal, fruit, and other drinks as desired. I knew the girls could handle it, but I did not want to explain why I was not there. With a quick dip in the shower, a fast hair comb, and a jump into my clothes, I was out the door and late by only fourteen minutes.

One of the older cooking assistants apparently suspected something and gave me a thumbs-up and a big grin as I cleared the kitchen door. But the others simply welcomed me with questions pertaining to the final breakfast preparation. I felt I was probably home safe.

Only a "short" later, personnel and patients began to appear at their tables, and the serving of breakfast moved into full swing. As usual Phil was one of the first to appear and was ready to be served. I allowed one of the other girls to serve him so it would not look so familiar.

Breakfast went off without a hitch, and everyone slowly moved away from the dining room back to their rooms or assignments.

After the cleanup detail was completed, one of the kitchen assistants remained behind and asked if she could have a few minutes of my time. Maria Aguilar appeared to be of Mexican or Central American descent. She was of a darker skin tone and had some American Indian facial features. I had talked to her earlier in her employment, and she told me she was with us to gain more experience in food preparation. She desired to someday become a top-level chef in a large eatery. Her full statement of origin was in her personnel file, but I had not read it in its entirety because I considered her to be temporary help. In a bold manner, she asked if she could sometime be completely in control of a meal preparation. She explained she had been studying Miss Jessie's preparation of old-south cuisine and felt she had a fair handle on that type of cooking. Now she would appreciate the opportunity to try out some southern border dishes on the personnel and patients to discover if she could develop some of that cuisine that would be liked and appreciated. She stated she understood the dishes would have to be modified to make them mild to the older residents' taste. But if she was successful it would enrich and broaden her cooking resume. She further explained that, like Miss Jessie, she had learned to cook regional food from her grandmother. And since Miss Jessie would be away for a while, could she try her hand with the food preparation?

I told her I would give it some thought and review her personnel file and if everything appeared as she presented it I would allow her an opportunity. However, I would be observing at all times. And to make that less stressful, if she proved to be a competent cook, I would add a positive statement to her personnel file.

When she turned to leave the kitchen I observed a huge smile as she graciously thanked me for my concern and patience.

Later when I reviewed her personnel file, I found a trove of interesting information. Her full name was Maria Elena Aguilar. She was born in El Paso, Texas, to illegal alien parents. They sometimes slipped across the border from Juarez, Mexico, into Texas to live and work as domestic laborers. She was born while they were living illegally in El Paso. Being born in the U. S., she was a legal citizen. Her parents, however, did not want to be listed as illegal persons in this country as they were attempting to gain legal status. When border problems came to the surface in the last few years, Maria stayed here and her parents went back to Mexico and hoped to emigrate sometime in the future. Her father was born in Honduras and her mother was born in Chihuahua, Mexico.

I would learn later still, when information came back from Country Freedom, that her great-grandfather was a revolutionary rider with Pancho Villa, and other relatives had been involved in lawless activities all through history up to the present time. Perhaps that was the reason her mother and father had been passed over several times on their request to legally emigrate.

Chapter 30

I should have realized he was an idiot! If he had done as I supposed he would, it would all be over. Otherwise I believe I've covered my track extremely well. The murderer mused, *I thought Billy would share his sweet powder with all his friends. I should have realized he would satisfy himself before he even remembered or thought about his close friends. When I saw him lace that bitch's dessert with the shaker, the taste of revenge was overwhelming in my mouth. I knew I had set up the perfect scenario—she would be done with and several others in her crowd would have bit the dust also. Then when he twisted that bitch around his finger and talked her into giving him her dessert, the whole damned scheme washed down the toilet.*

After a longer thought, the killer continued to evaluate the situation. *But of course the plan is not all lost. I have to doubt I'm even still a suspect. After the tale I told that worthless excuse for a female, she probably believes I'm the sweet, meek character I have portrayed. That dumb fair-haired excuse for a doctor certainly believed I was incapable of doing what I know I have to do. Oh well, at least that Ashfort moron will not get in the way the next time. The fact is I will probably hire someone else to do the job, and I won't even be the least involved. And...I damned sure will have an airtight alibi.*

With those sweet dreams of success playing in the mind of Billy's killer, there was a deeply felt sense of contentment. With a nod of the head the malcontent headed back to the assigned duties.

As each chore was completed, all thoughts continued to return of the hurt felt. Revenge! Memories of all the things lost kept going over and over in the mind as the desire rose higher and higher—REVENGE! The reward could not come soon enough.

79

Chapter 31

As the situation evolved, I continued to feel the heavy responsibility weighing me down. Phil was carrying his part, but I missed the constant support of the former five old buds. Of course Philo, as everyone else believed, was at eternal rest in the front garden. Thank God, Phil was really near and knew how to handle most of the situations. However, the remaining four were in and out for various lengths of time taking care of their own business domains.

John Niles was totally, head to tail, back into the computer universe. When he wasn't installing computer networks, he was designing and building new computer hardware and software.

Sandy Gallman, like Niles, was doing blueprints for huge electrical installations and selling electrical materials at the same time.

Leo Smiley had become involved in politics. As a lawyer, he did not want anyone else to experience the nightmares he and the rest of the buds had lived through. He was helping pass laws to protect old people from being railroaded into destruction at the hands of friends or relatives who wanted to steal their fortunes.

Ralph Cramp was the only one remaining most of the time at Knight's Gate. I liked to believe he had accepted me as his daughter and did not intend to allow me to be hurt ever again. But, his age slowly crept into his activities as he became more and more one of the patients at Knight's Gate instead of an owner. He still filled in as the overseer when I had to be out of the building. I tried to keep those times at a minimum. And I had to be very careful as he desired to know about everything that was happening. I told him the facts most of the time, but I protected him from the worst as much as I could. If he suspected I had held something back from him, his feelings were easily hurt.

The Ashfort murder had hurt all of us in some way. When Noah was destroyed we all thought the horror of Knight's Gate was over. But we were still facing danger and perhaps more horror. So, all we could do at the time was depend on Phil's knowledge, Country Freedom, and our own willpower to see us through. At the same time, deep in my heart I knew if it became necessary the old buds would all come together to defend the Gate on all fronts.

Phil and I continued our relationship as the home continued to try to meet the needs of the old gentlemen who had come there to make their final homes. We knew there was a killer among us, but we had no way of finding out who until more information was uncovered. Phil and I felt that all the known facts, so far, indicated I was the intended victim. This caused me some distress, but for Phil it was twice the pressure because he felt it was entirely his responsibility to keep me and the old gentlemen safe.

However, Phil found it was vastly important for him to keep a sense of humor and balance as he once more made it a point to try to take some of the pressure off me. Just hours before he'd slipped a note in my door's mail slot. It was a section of toilet tissue marked with three x's and the letters PTG, three kisses and a reminder to play the game. That gesture pumped me a great deal, and I'm sure gave Phil a lift at the same time.

Chapter 32

For a couple of weeks things seemed to simmer at a low temperature. Country Freedom was rechecking and reevaluating all the information that was available. Phil and I kept our feelings on hold except for a few minutes here and there. Phil made a daily report via the short-wave radio transmissions to his associate on the outside, and it was relayed to his section's headquarters. Business at the Gate ran as smoothly as if nothing unusual was going on; then it happened. Phil received word from Country Freedom that someone on the dark side was seeking a paid assailant for a job in Galeton, Illinois. His organization zeroed in on the communication with all its facilities and finances. As we suspected the intelligence seemed to be centered around Knight's Gate Retirement Home for Mature Gentlemen. So it seemed our killer was searching for outside help to accomplish his or her mission. We knew Miss Jessie was being held in such a way that it would have been almost impossible for her to seek such assistance. But stranger things have proven, in the past, to be possible, so she was still not completely out of the woods. All the other suspects had freedom to roam on and off campus, so anyone could be the culprit. Country Freedom immediately asked Phil if he desired to be put up as a candidate for the paid hit job.

I knew the answer before Phil opened his mouth. That was his specialty, and with Knight's Gate and me being the target of the assassin, he would be prepared in moments. I felt my whole world spinning out of control, but it was the most fortunate break we had been given. As I tried to convince him not to put himself in danger, he retorted that he and I were already in extreme danger. And that a break of such magnitude would give him the chance to bring the whole affair to an end. But, I gave my argument one more try: "This means you might have to kill again or be killed in the activity."

83

Then he had one more piece of defense: "Ab', your father, Blank's grandfather, Philo, and Billy have all paid the price. I could never live a normal life with you if I willingly allowed anyone else to perish. Especially, I couldn't go on living if the next victim were you." Then he kissed me; he had evidently made his final decision.

Chapter 33

Because of the sudden intrusion caused by the news from Country Freedom and Phil's declaration, my concentration was fractured. But, trying to keep things operating at the Gate, I suddenly remembered I had promised Maria Aguilar I would consider her request to totally run the kitchen for one meal of Tex-Mex cuisine. I checked the calendar for a couple of weeks and found a Sunday evening dinner slot I felt would fit the bill for the attention Maria desired.

I called the young lady into my office and presented my offer. With a huge grin she thanked me and then began to question what she would have to do for supplies and which patients had special needs. I assured her all supplies would be furnished by Knight's Gate, but she would be responsible for researching the home's records to learn the exact needs of each of our residents with special dietary demands. I explained that in that way she would be forced to realize the needs of all her future restaurant customers.

As we spoke, a light appeared in her eyes as she asked, "Ms. Jordan, could we have a small fiesta along with the meal? We could have games and party favors for the old gentlemen. Perhaps some would even enjoy dressing in jeans and colorful shirts for the occasion. Since it's to be on a Sunday evening, it could be a very special holiday celebration. Ms. Jordan, I and some of the other girls could do all the work, and maybe I could find some clothing at Goodwill to use as costumes."

I thought for a moment and then answered, "Maria, plan it out and write a proposal so I can look at all you plan, and then I will give the okay if everything is...okay." As she left my office I believed she was walking several inches above the floor. I was happy that some pleasure could be found inside the Gate's walls, if only for a little while. And, it also gave me some pleasure as I thought of some costume I could wear reflecting a Latin theme.

A short time later, Maria presented me with a very well-done menu and plans for a mini fiesta. After reading her plan I was extremely satisfied with her work. So, in writing, I gave my permission to proceed with a promise of a written letter in her personnel file if the celebration was a success.

Phil was extremely busy planning his performance if he was called to take the job as the paid assailant against Knight's Gate and me. But he also took time to prepare for the celebration. I believed he wanted us to enjoy every moment we could, in case the unthinkable happened. I kept telling myself he was a pro and nothing could go wrong, but I also knew he was not necessarily infallible. However, while he and I were meeting every moment with a form of dread, the rest of Knight's Gate was living at the height of anticipation. Even Dan was looking forward as he quietly told me, "Miss Abby, the bastards won't get me before the fiesta!" And I really believed he was going to prove to be correct.

Finally the Sunday rolled around and Maria was the toast of the residence. All day she was dressed as a high-level Mexican lady, a doña of a wealthy hacienda, with her dress, fans, combs, and beautiful coal-black hair. All the young men paid close attention to her every move. I felt a little sorry for Peggy Duff—Robert Kobb was almost completely ignoring her as his total attention seemed to be on Maria. But at the dinner hour Maria appeared in a complete white chef's uniform along with the tall puffed hat completing the ensemble. She was totally in charge of the kitchen and the food preparation, and everyone at the Gate knew it.

Most of the rest of the attendants were wearing various pieces of clothing denoting the southern border of the United States. Even Robert Kobb attempted to meet the requirement. He appeared in a worn white high school sweatshirt with the words San Benito, Texas "Fleas" in bright red letters emblazoned across the chest. He also sported a pair of tan football practice shorts and red-and-gold striped gym socks. Phil asked him what it all meant, and he replied, "San Benito is a small town—so small our mascot is a flea." Everyone began to laugh, and he continued, "My home town is only a few miles from Harlingen and the border town of Matamoros. So I guessed I would fit into a Mexican fiesta." He saluted and went looking for Peggy Duff, I assumed to make amends for his all-day actions concerning Maria.

The banquet started at about 6 p.m. Maria and her staff had prepared carne asada as the main course, and the beef was as tender as angel food cake after being marinated in papaya juice. Then it was once more marinated in a pasilla chile–based sauce, grilled over hot coals until nearly burned, and served with a salsa of combined citrus and more pasilla. As a refreshing lead dish, she chose sopa de tortilla. The course consisted of corn tortilla strips in a chicken broth seasoned with tomatoes and pasilla chiles then served with avocado, queso, and crema (cheese and cream). Guacamole and tortilla chips were served alongside. The avocado was a muted green color with hefty chucks of tomato and onion with just a taste of lime juice. A second side dish was caldo de pollo—bits of tender chicken with vegetables, fire-roasted tomatoes, and sweet corn. As a delicious dessert finish to the meal, buñuelos with fresh honey were delivered. Soft drinks, coffee, and hibiscus tea—hot or iced—were also served. To honor Miss Jessie's southern specialties, rich mashed potatoes with heavy butter and garlic were also served on request.

After the meal some simple games were played and costumes were judged. Merriment continued until most of the older guests appeared to become weary. At about 8 p.m., the festivities came to an end as the residents moved back to their rooms and the attendants began to clean and prepare for Monday morning.

Maria's day was a total success, and I was extremely proud to know I owed her a letter of commendation to go into her personnel file. But first, I located her in the kitchen, wearing scrubs, doing her part to get the place shipshape for the next day. "Maria, today was a fine piece of work, and I want to congratulate you on a job well done."

She immediately ran to me and gave me a huge hug. "Ms. Jordan, you are the first one in my life to really believe I was capable of something such as this. Thank you so much for giving me the chance."

Phil got close enough to me to whisper and suggested a little R and R for a couple of hours before we had to call it a night and prepare for a new week. In extreme relief I agreed as we stole away to his off-campus apartment for a little wine and a lot of love.

Chapter 34

A couple of days after the fiesta I was working at my desk and became a little fatigued at the job I was working on, so I decided to take a short break. I suddenly remembered Robert Kobb saying he was from San Benito, Texas. Wondering just where that little town was in the great state of Texas, I ran the name up on the World Wide Web. As Robert had said, it was a town close to the Mexican border near Harlingen, Texas. The city of San Benito had a small home page, so I read its reviews. It had a moderate football program, and its mascot was the "Fighting Flea." I got a charge out of that piece of information. Secondly it was a farming community with its share of Mexican labor crossing the border to work the farms. That was not earth-shattering news as most of the U.S. border areas depended on cross-over labor. Then I read the tourist information and found they had a nice golf course that was recognized as a destination course to play. The ad stated that golfers from all over Texas and other nearby states traveled there to play the "Benito Greens," and that Casa Santos was a five-star eating establishment in the area. I finished the home page with a smile on my face and returned to the work at hand.

Later at dinner I happened to mention that young Kobb was a real asset to the Gate's staff. He was knowledgeable, a steady worker, and had a very happy demeanor. I had to laugh as I explained I had done some research on San Benito, and it wasn't much unless you counted the golf course and the eating joint, Casa Santos. Phil was just answering his phone and didn't pay much attention to what I was saying, so I concentrated more on the delicious food the girls had prepared. Old-fashioned vegetable soup is my favorite, and theirs was made the way I really liked it.

In a few moments Phil was off the phone and asked what I had been saying. I told him it was not that important and to concentrate on his meal. The other option for the evening meal was red meat, and Phil certainly loved red meat of any kind, so we were both happy with the fare. And then it was the same question: Was I ready for a little time away from the Gate? He was planning to spend the night on-site but needed some fresh clothes, so he was going to the apartment if I cared to ride along. I definitely had the desire to have him alone for a few minutes or several hours, whatever amount of time we could steal. In a few minutes we were gone, and I didn't care when we returned. I dearly loved *our* time.

Chapter 35

After a period of time Phil received the message via a creature of the street that he, as Paul, was hired to fulfill a contract on a person residing at Knight's Gate Retirement Home for Mature Gentlemen. He immediately began planning all the activities that would enable him to be away from Knight's Gate for a while. He needed time to form a cover story, so he decided he would go to a medical convention or fulfill a previous commitment in another city. He and Country Freedom finally settled on a need to return to his previous employment to testify in a lawsuit having to do with some irregular activities committed by some of his previous associates, perhaps leading to some bankruptcy proceedings. He assured me that all the records were in place that, if necessary, would prove he was on company business during his absence.

After informing as many of our personnel as he deemed necessary to assure they knew he was going and what he would be doing, he and I brazenly took a weekend off together to take a small trip to Chicago. Pleasantly, no one seemed to be shocked or offended by our bold plan, so, taking my car, we drove away to enjoy every minute we could have together.

Our little love trip was enjoyable from a tourist point of view as well as the hours we had together, just the two of us. During the day it was museums, fine food, shopping, and chill time, while at night, it was nothing but love. My first marriage was very satisfying until the divorce, but this little trip was above and beyond any time I spent with my first husband. Phil was all mine, and he did everything to prove it. The only down side to the whole affair was when it ended on Sunday evening as we drove back to Galeton.

As he helped me unload my suitcase and other personal items, he told me he would not see me for a while as it was time for him to establish his identity in some other location. I would not be able to visit, but he would let me know where he was. I would be the only one who would know.

I kissed him as he prepared to get into the taxi that would take him to the supposed airport for his journey to his old work place. And then he was gone.

A little later as I looked around Knight's Gate, searching for something to occupy my mind other than worrying about Phil, an idea came to mind. Phil and I had dismissed Samson Mann as the most unlikely candidate for being the murderer. But, thinking like Phil, I suddenly realized the least likely candidate could very well be the most likely suspect. So...I decided to just visit Mr. Mann and see for myself who he was and what he was doing. A visit from the head of the facility couldn't be construed as anything other than a business concern. That's not to say I did not know Samson; I just never had reason to meet him one-on-one before.

As I walked down the hall toward his room I knew I needed a reason for making an appearance at that particular moment. Then I vaguely remembered one of the attendants had said he had developed an illness that caused him to spend a lot of time in his room, often requiring his food to be delivered to his room at meal time. At that moment I knew I had a reasonable concern to go to his room.

When I reached his room, the door was open into the hall. I looked in and Samson was propped up in bed having a bite of Sunday-evening dinner. When he saw me a smile slowly spread across his face. "Ms. Jordan, how can I be of service to you?"

Before I answered I quickly looked him and the room over. "Mr. Mann, I heard you have been ill, but not seriously. I've been away from Knight's Gate for the weekend and decided as soon as I returned I needed to personally check up on you. And now here I am. What's wrong and how are you feeling?"

"Nothing serious, just some bug that has a bite of my tail and won't turn loose. I have these things sometimes and they eat on me for weeks, even a month or more at various times. I'll be okay now that Dr. Phil is in charge. He is one heck of a doctor. I came down with this bug a few days before Mr. Ashfort died and Dr. Phil has been trying to get me well enough to get out of this bed and back into the sunshine. He says he believes I may be up and around in a few more days. Can't wait to get back outside in the sun."

"Samson, you be careful of that old sunshine; it can hurt you bad if it's too hot."

"That's okay, Ms. Jordan. I always keep myself well hibernated, so I'm not worried about that."

"Don't you mean you keep yourself well hydrated?"

"Nope! Well hibernated. I sleep like a log every time I close my eyes. Fact is, that's how I'm able to stay in this danged bed so long." And with that statement he loudly laughed until tears came to his eyes.

Then I realized he had not been out of his room the day Billy died, so I decided to remove him from the list of suspects for good. Or until some unbelievable fact appeared to prove otherwise. Bidding him good night, I left his room and headed back to my apartment and back to my worries about Phil.

Chapter 36

With Phil in hiding waiting for directions from the killer, and I being the supposed victim, I did not believe things around me could get any worse. But they could.

On a morning when I was deep in more of my hated paperwork, one of the young male attendants rushed into my office with a look of deep fear in his eyes. "Ms. Jordan, I believe it best that you go with me to the ladies' room in the other wing!"

Before I could ask what reason I would have to accompany him to the ladies' room, he continued, "Two of the female medical assistants have locked themselves in, and very uncivilized words are flowing between them. I heard one even say something about kicking the other one's tail till her nose bled. I don't know what is going on, but I believe they intend to hurt each other."

Grabbing the master key, I rushed out of the office ahead of the young man and made a bee line for the ladies' restroom. When I arrived, I also heard words even rougher than the ones the young man reported. One of the young ladies had graduated to calling the other a filthy whore. At that point I felt the word battle had gone far enough, and I was not waiting for the physical part to start.

"YOUNG LADIES, OPEN THE DOOR IMMEDIATELY!"

For a few moments the area became silent...and then I heard solid bone meet flesh and I used the pass key to gain entry into the bathroom.

Sitting on the floor holding her stomach was Stephanie James, one of the Giggling Girls. A little way away was Jeanie Pratt, another of the medical assistants, standing in a classic boxing pose with one fist positioned in defense and the other ready to land another blow. "I said I'd kick her ass and now I've done it and I'm not sorry! She's trying to take my man and no damned woman is going to take the man I love and am going to marry!"

Then a loud howl came from the little woman on the floor. "You bitch, he's going to marry me!"

Then I broke into the filthy dispute: "Who is going to marry whom, I beg to know?"

In duet they both howled at the same moment, "Hector is going to marry me!" And then they dove for each other again. The young male attendant and I each grabbed one of the little monkeys and held on for dear life. After struggling for a few long moments both relaxed, and I felt the battle was over.

Then from the open door, where a small crowd of curious gawkers had gathered, came a meek little voice from the back of the crowd, from a person I could not see. "They're both liars; Hector is going to marry me as soon as his divorce is final." The crowd parted, and I saw the little round body of Joy Nokowski, another of the gigglers. She had her feet spread apart with her hands on her hips and her lip stuck out a mile. And she was nodding her head.

The young male attendant and I grabbed the other two girls tightly one more time as they both started to lunge at Joy. Then they all howled at once, "He's mine and no one else is going to get him!"

I looked around and saw two more of my young male attendants and asked them to hold the one I had, and the other grabbed Joy. Then I was able to step back, catch my breath, and try to decide how to defuse the whole stinking mess.

Then, as my eyes panned the surroundings, I caught sight of Hector Ross standing at the far back of the onlookers. "HECTOR, GET UP HERE RIGHT NOW!"

Perhaps a little sheepishly he sauntered to the front of the crowd. As he walked forward, I saw him look over at the three girls, and a snide grin appeared on his face. I had thought to scold him a little in front of the girls, but I thought better of it and decided to talk to him one-on-one in my office. "Mr. Ross, please meet me in my office in a couple of minutes." With that, he slowly moved down the hall toward my door.

The girls had seemed to settle down a little, so I told the young attendants to turn them loose. They each headed away in separate directions—one down the hall and one up the hall as the third waited until the crowd scattered.

As I entered my office, I found Hector in my chair with his feet on my desk.

"MOVE IT, KID!"

He dropped his feet and quickly stood up.

In a flash, I made up my mind. "Mr. Ross, I believe it best if you pick up your personal materials and vacate Knight's Gate immediately. You can pick up your final pay tomorrow morning in my office."

Slowly his demeanor quieted, and he asked, "Ms. Jordan, why are you firing me when I'm doing nothing different than you and your make-believe doctor? All I was doing was having a little sexual fun with the bodies at hand."

"What do you mean, make-believe doctor?"

"I've been in a lot of these joints, and your squeeze is no more a doctor than I am. What's the game—do you pay him as a bed partner because you're so old you can't get a man any other way? And besides all that, if you push this and cause me trouble, I'll talk some of the old shits here into bringing charges against you and your so-called doctor—illegal medical practice without a license."

With those words said, I only asked two more questions: "Are you serious about any one of the three girls, and are you married?"

"Hell no. Look at me. With my looks I can have any woman I want! Fact is, I've been married several times."

Then I broke, "Hell no, you can't. Not me and not any of my girls if I can find someone to help keep you away from them. Like my make-believe doctor for one, and Detective Bradley Blank, for a second. NOW, GET OUT!"

As he left my office, I almost felt dirty by association.

Chapter 37

I hadn't seen Phil for several days as he had taken up residence in one of the low-class motels in the seedy part of Galeton. He made the move to remain unseen by his dark-side employers so they could not discover his actual identity. But he felt the killer would be present at the Gate when he appeared, to celebrate their revenge, whoever they were. He told me to contact Brad Blank and tell him I was getting anxious about being the target for the next murder and that he had been called away to an important meeting and would not be around to protect me. But, we still had the buzzer system if I was attacked. He also told me he had disabled all the buzzers except Blank's. Then he ended the conversation by telling me I would hear the whole story after the mess was all over.

Still realistically being scared beyond imagination, I decided I had to rely on Phil and the detective to keep me safe. Actually, the more I thought about it the better I felt. If the killer was hiring a hit man and the hit man was Phil, then evidently the killer did not plan to hurt me but would let Phil do the dirty work. I did wonder what the plan was to do away with me. But I tried to put it all out of my mind as I went back to the work at hand.

I met with Cramp and explained it was going to be he and I for a few days as Phil was out of town. Ralph actually did a little jig and replied, "Abby, it's going to be like old times—you and me keeping this business running. I hope you don't mind that I'm looking forward to it!" I assured him I was also happy we could have some time to party and joke without any interference.

But, it seemed that at the moment I needed to keep my wits about me: pressing problems arose once more. Almost immediately after the dinner hour Dan Herdon experienced another few moments of not breathing and scared me almost to distraction. When I got to his room, Robert Kobb had beat me to his side and was administering treatment and monitoring Dan's oxygen intake. And thankfully Dan was breathing once more in his rough sort of way as his face returned to a pink color from the white countenance I observed as I entered his room. I immediately thanked Robert for his work and God for the medical expertise the young man demonstrated. When Dan finally recognized who I was, he smiled weakly and immediately went to sleep. I felt a great deal of gratitude that we had a fine young man like Robert on our staff. I went back to my rooms and felt we were in safe hands with young Kobb on the job.

The next morning at breakfast Robert, before he went off duty, approached me and asked if I would be bothered if he contacted me in the evening hours should Dan appear to be in distress. He stated he felt he could handle most situations, but he would like for me to be present if Dan's condition became dangerous. I assured him all he had to do was knock at my door and I would join him if necessary, or if the situation was critical, he could just send someone else to get me while he continued to care for Dan. He thanked me and exited the building for his day of rest.

A little later in the morning, Phil called to tell me if the meeting went well he would probably return in the evening today or perhaps tomorrow. I told him I would be waiting, and we simply said good bye.

I quickly reran his call through my mind and determined this must be the day he was expected to make his attack on me. But, what do we do if the killer does not come forward at the same time? I was rapidly coming apart at the seams when a simple statement ran through my mind: *Abby, just play the game.* I had to believe Phil had it set up in such a way that it would work out exactly the way it was meant to be. I swallowed a number of times and then continued my day as though it was any other day in the life of Abigail Jordan.

Chapter 38

As the day wore on I became more and more agitated. I was scared and feared everyone around me. I hid in my rooms as much as I could because I was afraid I would divulge to someone what was going to happen, and I was scared they might be the killer. I thought about talking to Cramp, but sadly I feared he might be the plant! How could I believe such nonsense?

I don't know how Phil accomplished the feat, but late in the afternoon after one of my few ventures out of my rooms, when I returned there was a toilet paper note in my mail slot. It read as follows:

"Tonight is the night. Earlier I looked in the newspaper and the coded message was there. I will get to your room after the killer gets there. Don't fear, I'll come in within a minute or two of the SOB's arrival. Of course you will recognize me as I will be dressed exactly as I was the night Crawford made his entry. DON'T GIVE US AWAY...ACT SCARED TO DEATH. And don't be surprised as to who the person turns out to be! I love you and if necessary I will die for you or with you. But I don't think it will come to that. As soon as you recognize who the killer is, press the buzzer to contact Blank, as he has already been prepped that this is the real thing. REMEMBER, DO NOT GIVE US AWAY TO ANYONE, NO MATTER HOW MUCH YOU TRUST THEM! XXX"

Now that the appointed hour had arrived, I was close to being a basket case. I thought I was extremely brave, but in the face of death once more, I was mostly mouse, not cat. But as I began to breathe

101

less rapidly I also became more relaxed and contained. Finally, knowing almost the exact time of the attack, I felt I now had some control over the situation. I had been hiding for such a long period of time I had become fearful of almost everything. So I decided since the time of my murder was to be later in the day, I had a few hours of freedom to do as I liked. Putting on a pair of comfortable shoes, I decided to take a walk in the outside air.

As I exited the building, no one seemed to pay much attention. I decided, to still remain safe, I would limit my walk to Knight's Gate's grounds. As I moved to the backyard area I remembered the lawn mower shed behind the row of shrubs, the shed where I found my father's and Mr. Calone's records. Walking in that direction, I suddenly remembered that when I found the records I had observed something else near the old sheet-metal shed, but at the time I was too distracted to give it much thought.

Directly behind the old shed I had found a patch of tilled soil. A garden plot about twelve by twenty feet in size, with tomatoes, onions, green peppers, and beans growing there. Also, at one corner of the plot were the large green leaves of a zucchini plant with a huge green squash on the ground beneath. At the same time, in a shady spot behind the back wall of the shed, I had seen an old worn plastic lawn chair. As my mind returned to the present, against the wall—still there after almost two years—stood a rusty old rake and hoe, but the old lawn chair was gone and Mother Nature had almost completely reclaimed the garden spot to return it to lawn.

Back at the earlier time, one of the older attendants told me that was George's garden. Some of the old workers called him George and others "Mr. T." I saw him only once at the garden plot. He was peacefully napping in the old chair, a simple man in a place for him, his God, and his garden.

I had not been at Knight's Gate very long before his family moved him to another nursing home because he needed more intensive care. George Thomas was a city man but thoroughly loved working in God's rich earth.

As my thoughts continued to wander, I felt thankful Mr. Thomas did not have the amount of wealth that had caused the death of my father and Mr. Calone. He simply needed a place and Knight's Gate was that place.

For some reason I began to feel fatigued as stress once more invaded my spirit, so I decided I needed to once more return to my room. But at the same time, I enjoyed the memory of an old man and his garden.

Once back in my room, to hopefully help settle my nerves a little, I turned on some soft stereo music and called the girls to inform them I would not appear for dinner as I was experiencing a minor headache and would be trying to sleep it off. I decided if I became hungry I would simply go to the kitchen and make a small sandwich or get perhaps a small bowl of soup. Then I curled up in one of the easy chairs in my main room and attempted to remain as calm as I could. I really needed to talk to Phil, but I knew it was not wise to break his train of thought this close to the event, and besides, our phones may have been tapped by the killer or perhaps an accomplice. It was down to me to buck up and play the game.

After what seemed to be ten hours the dinner hour arrived. I decided I was so stressed I would simply skip eating. I supposed I was a little hungry, but I didn't believe I could eat anything at all. Then it was back to the long wait once again.

***

She eased up the hall toward Abby's apartment, being very careful not to be seen. She knew she had waited much too long to get done what had to be done. The necessity brought a sour taste up into her throat. But she was determined this was the time and the place to bring the whole rotten thing to a close.

As she neared Abby's door she heard light footsteps coming around the corner from the opposite direction. Pressing herself as flat as she could against the nearest door, she hoped the door frame and facing would hide her from the approaching eyes. Then she saw Robert Kobb face Abby's door and rap lightly. *Damn,* she thought. *Don't tell me I have to do this all over again later!*

***

I must have dozed a little because I became aware that there was someone tapping on my door. I looked up at the sun blaze clock above my tiny fireplace and was surprised—it displayed 10:45. I walked to the door and asked who it was. Robert Kobb answered and said he needed to talk to me about Dan. When I knew it was Robert I relaxed a little as he was such a nice young man. I opened the door, and he asked to come in. Then I was scared again. What if the killer came in while Robert was with me. I didn't want him in danger, but I didn't know how to turn him away. Not knowing what else to do, I invited him in.

"Ms. Jordan, Dan had another episode tonight. I believe he's okay now, that's why I came to tell you. One of the other guys is with him now, so you needn't worry. I just felt you should know."

***

Kobb had entered Abby's apartment, but before she could move away from her hiding place in the door frame another figure appeared in front of Abby's door. The figure moved so fast and so smoothly that she almost did not see it at all. Strange! The figure was dressed in a tight black body suit, including the head. She could not tell if the figure was male or female. With a fluid motion the figure unlocked Abby's door and disappeared inside. Not waiting to determine what was happening next, she hurried away to find a place to hide. Her last thought at that moment was, *Maybe I can get enough strength to try tomorrow.*

***

Suddenly the door opened and a slight figure slid inside. The person was dressed in a tight-fitting black ninja costume with all body parts covered except for the eyes. In their hand was the same small wicked-looking black dagger I remembered from the attack by Oscar Crawford over a year before. I immediately recognized Phil, but I feigned extreme fear as I threw my hands up in front of my face and backed up a step or two.

Then Robert Kobb's personality change drastically, and his face took on a twisted evil appearance as he screamed at me, "Now you're going to get yours, bitch! I've been patiently waiting all these days, weeks, and months to see this moment come. You're so damned high and mighty. You beat a man to death and then you're made out to be some kind of hero. Well, now it's your turn to take a beating... until you're dead, just like my brother. Oh, I know he wasn't worth much to you, but he was my big brother, my hero. And you...you bitch, killed him in cold blood. If that stupid little idiot Billy had had just a little brain power, the poison would have got you a long time ago. Now, my man here has been paid big money to beat you to death slowly just like my brother. Paul, I'm going to get back to work so I won't be a suspect, and you get her out of here and do your thing." Then Robert turned and exited my rooms and I supposed headed back to Dan's room.

As soon as the door closed and locked, Phil removed his garb and stuffed it into a throw-pillow sham and tossed it onto one of the easy chairs and then rapidly combed his hair. As he was taking care of himself he told me to quickly trip the buzzer for Blank to arrive. Then he kissed me as he slid out the door.

Almost before I could catch my breath, there was another knock at my door, and I recognized Brad Blank's voice as he demanded, "Abby, are you in there? Are you okay?"

When I unlocked the door, he was standing there with his pistol in his hand, and two well-armed men in riot gear were right behind him. "Did someone try to harm you tonight? I got an anonymous tip earlier that you would be attacked tonight by Billy's killer. Has he or she been here?"

I asked him to come into my apartment, and then I explained the whole thing. I told him the guilty party was Robert Kobb, one of our young attendants. But I told him I did not understand the reason he kept repeating. I explained that Robert said I had beaten his older brother to death and he was going to exact revenge and have me beaten to death by a paid third party.

"Was the third party here tonight?" I nodded my head as he continued, "Who was it and where are they now?"

I continued to explain that they were both here in my room and Robert went back, I assumed, to Dan Herdon's room so he would not be a suspect. After that the paid killer simply ran away. Then I adlibbed a little as I said, "I guess there's no honor among criminals. The killer got paid in advance, so he just took the money and ran. But Robert Kobb did admit in front of me that he was the one who gave the poison to Billy, so I suppose you have the killer right here for the taking."

"Where is Dan's room? We'll just go get the little skunk right now."

Quietly we moved out of my rooms and walked down the halls to Dan's room. I waited outside as the three lawmen walked in the door and rapidly put young Kobb under arrest for the murder of Billy Ashfort.

As Robert was led out of the room with his hands cuffed behind his back, he saw me and a wild puzzlement crossed his face. "You bitch, why aren't you dead? I paid big money to that cheap bastard to kill you." As tears filled his eyes he quietly said, "You can't trust anyone."

Then it was my turn to ask a question. "Robert, how could I have killed your brother? I don't even know another man named Kobb."

"His name was Santos...Carlo Santos. He was my half-brother. We had the same mother, but his father was part of the family that owns Casa Santos in my hometown. My father is a lawyer in San Benito, and you'll be hearing from him." But then Kobb's expression changed again as he boasted, "I did get that other bastard though, that Philo, the dumb-headed prick, my man in Chicago, blew his dumb ass to kingdom come."

With that final declaration, Brad Blank and the other officers escorted Robert toward the door and then to their waiting patrol van. As they exited the front door, Phil came running in through the same door. He was bellowing at the top of his voice, "Abby, Abby, are you here, are you okay? God help me, tell me you're okay."

As I stepped out into the middle of the hallway he saw me and pulled me to him. We stood there for a few moments for all to see, and then we returned to my rooms. As we closed the door, I found one of the easy chairs and simply collapsed. After a few moments I raised my head, and he asked once more, "Are you okay now that this damned nightmare is really over?"

I nodded my head as he kissed me and slid out the door, explaining he would be in his room on the premises. I didn't argue; I simply stumbled into the bedroom and fell onto the bed.

When I awoke the next morning, I don't believe I ha
more than a couple of inches all night. After a quick sho
cleanup I was ready for the day. I had so much to do. First t.
to tell Cramp what had happened and then to check with
Miss Jessie could return to work. And then, if Blank said (
call Miss Jessie Crum and tell her to get her butt back to the
quickly as she could. I loved and missed that woman.

But before I could even get started, Rose Mary Smith co
me as I tried to turn the corner toward the dining hall. My bra
screaming for coffee, and it was all I could do to keep from p
her out of the way and continuing on to my waiting treasure.

"Ms. Jordan, please, please, I have to talk to you right nc
don't talk now I'll never be able to tell you, and I'm so mixed u
scared I'll just run away."

"I take it you would like to speak to me privately?"

"Yes, please. I'm afraid my heart will break if I can't co.
right now!"

"Okay, allow me time to get my coffee, and we'll go to my r
and talk."

"Oh, thank you, Ms. Jordan."

She remained in the hall while I filled my cup, took a
satisfying drink, and then refilled the cup. Then we hurried t
apartment.

Chapter 39

Almost before we were comfortably seated, Rose Mary started to talk. It was almost as if she would die if she did not clear her mind.

"I was outside your door last night and I saw Robert enter your apartment, then in a moment someone else entered. That person was strangely dressed and scared me. As soon as I could I ran to one of the empty exercise rooms and hid. I didn't come out until daylight. Then I heard everyone talking about Robert being arrested for Billy's murder. I was still scared to death for you until someone said you and Dr. Phil were okay. But there's so much more I need to tell you. Ms. Jordan, I lied about myself. Part of what I said earlier was true, but I lied. I said I came to work here because my father said you ran a great organization. That part is the truth. But I really came here to try to discover if my father was involved in any mischief at Knight's Gate. After his death, I know everyone heard on the national news he was a dirty politician. I was really hurt by those accusations, and I could not believe he was not being soiled by jealous rivals. But, when his estate was settled and I discovered he was worth several million dollars, I was flabbergasted. As a professional working woman, I knew an honest man could not make that amount of money on even a top-level politician's salary. Sadly, I had to believe he was dirty. Then I remembered as I was growing up, he would sometimes say rules and laws are made to allow the control of people who are not smart enough to take care of themselves. But if you are smart enough you can work outside the boundaries and become very successful. Ms. Jordan, I'm afraid he was far outside the boundaries when he died. Then when Billy was murdered and it was said you were the target, I knew you would find out I was Oscar Crawford's daughter and you would believe I was as dirty as my father. Ms. Jordan, I love working here and working for you, so I hope you will never believe

I'm anything but an honest nurse trying to help people stay alive. I could never willingly harm anyone."

At that moment I, like Phil, believed she was the real thing. I believed it because she told me, and Phil believed it because he saw her do her job. Though I didn't tell her, I knew Oscar Crawford was a rat, but I believed his daughter was a lovable pussycat. I thanked her for her openness and then I asked, "Nurse Smith, don't you have some sweet old men who are waiting for the touch of your hand?"

"Yes, Ms. Jordan, and I'm on my way. Thank you!"

She disappeared down the hallway, and I returned to my planned activities.

Chapter 40

After a quick breakfast, as quick as it could be after having the conversation with Nurse Smith and answering all the questions about the night before, I cornered Cramp and explained all that had happened. With a look of relief, he stated, "I'm glad this mess is finally over. We're almost all still alive, and it appears the last of Noah is out of the picture. Perhaps we can now all grow old together and leave this world naturally."

I patted his shoulder and whispered, "Now perhaps Philo can also rest in peace."

I saw a tear trickle down his cheek as he replied, "I really miss that little shit. He wasn't much, but he was a lot more human than many of the people we have come in contact with the last couple of years."

Then I asked, "Do we need to contact the other three buds to tell them what has happened?"

With a look of resignation he touched my arm and answered, "Not really; they are completely back in their own worlds and living totally free. If they come around we can always tell them the main facts and continue to live our lives clean and free also."

Then without hesitation I did something I had never done before. I stood on tiptoe and kissed the old man on the cheek and lightly said, "Thank you for all you are and have been to me, Dad."

With more tears on his face he whispered, "Abby, thank you you are more my flesh and blood than anyone else I've ever known."

Giving him one more pat on the shoulder I turned and headed down the hall to complete my morning chores. It took a few minutes, but I was finally able to speak to Brad Blank on the phone. I simply asked him if he thought it would be okay for Miss Jessie to come back to work.

Without any thought, he replied, "Get that woman back where she belongs. I can't wait to dig into more of her fine food."

Hanging up quickly, I immediately dialed Jessie's number and heard her ask, "Ms. Jordan, will I ever get to come back to work? I'm so lonely and blue I don't think I'll ever be well again."

"Miss Jessie, how long would it take for you to arrive at the Gate if I told you to come to work right now?"

She answered, "Miss Abby, if you told me that, you could look out your office window and I would be standing there."

"Then you had better appear in about two seconds, because I need you now."

"Oh, thank you, Miss Abby. It will take a little longer than that, but I'm on my way!"

As I hung up the phone, I felt so good inside myself. Then it was time to see old Dan and explain what had transpired during the night. So I locked my door and headed down the hall to his room.

Chapter 41

As I entered Dan's room, his eyes followed my approach to his bed. When I was very close to him he spoke in a sound I could barely hear. Reaching out for my hand, he began to whisper. "Miss Abby, I have been holding on for quite a long time. I knew there was," then there was a long pause before he was able to continue, "I knew there was a snake still within these walls." Another pause and then, "But I didn't know who. Now he has been found out." Another pause, longer this time. "I'm just so sorry it was young Kobb. He had the makings of a fine medical man." Closing his eyes, I thought perhaps he was going to sleep, but after yet another pause, he took a deep ragged breath and finished. "Thank you for caring for me, but now I can go on when I'm called." After a moment he began to snore peacefully.

After leaving Dan's room I decided it was time to talk to Phil and get the whole story. Or, get the parts of the story I had not been privy to. I found him in the old room he had occupied as Philo. Being polite, I softly knocked on the door. He opened the door dressed in his red-and-black robe and fuzzy white slippers, with a cup of coffee in his hand.

"I figured as soon as you forced the lid back on Knight's Gate you would be coming around to get the whole scoop. Come and sit on the couch with me, and I will attempt to clue you in. But, I demand to know what has happened at your end."

"Phil, please explain to me all that happened at your end first."

After a moment or two to align his thoughts, Phil began to speak. "As you already knew, I was contracted by someone to kill you. The only thing they did not know was I was on your side. I accepted the contract and the person paying for it wanted to be present to declare revenge. When I walked into your apartment, Kobb was already there as per the plan."

Then I butted in, "But when you came in, weren't you surprised that Kobb was the one there?"

"No. I already had a good idea he was the one."

"How? I would have never dreamed it was him."

"Abby, you were the one with the answer, you just didn't realize you had it."

"What? What did I know that I didn't realize?"

"At dinner you talked about Kobb's hometown of San Benito, and how it had a golf course and a fine eating place—Casa Santos. Do you know what Casa Santos means in English?"

"Of course, it's the house or home of Santos."

"Didn't that ring a bell? Carlo Santos was the man who was going to kill you a year and a half ago."

"Yes, I knew that, but I just supposed it was a coincidence that both names were the same."

"Well yes, I'll have to give you that, but I knew one thing you didn't know. In Santos's records that was found in his rental, here in Galeton, with all the other material, was a form with his home address on it. That home address was San Benito, Texas. And if you remember, he tried to get Miss Jessie's job as the food specialist here at Knight's Gate but was told Miss Jessie was a very satisfactory chef. He evidently felt he could cook for a large group or he would not have asked about the job. Casa Santos is a very large eatery where he would have learned to cook for large groups."

I felt quite foolish as Phil explained that, but I realized then that Phil's training never allowed anyone to assume there was a coincidence.

"Ab', after those two pieces were in place I went back and researched and found that Kobb's mom was married twice. First she was married to Don Juan Santos and had a son—Carlo. After Juan was killed in an act of mob violence she married Robert Kobb Sr., and they had a son–Robert Jr. Oh yes, and Casa Santos is a mob haven and has been for many, many years."

"Now it all fits...but do you think this mess is finally, completely over, or will we see more and more from the remains of the Noah Cartel?"

"It would appear it's behind us unless Rose Mary Smith comes to the surface in some way."

Then I told him of my conversation with Rose Mary, and that I did not believe she would ever be a problem. And I also told him of my short talk with Dan Herdon and said that I did not believe he would be a problem either. Finally I told him of my talk with Blank and that Miss Jessie was coming back. That is, if she wasn't already in the building.

"Ab', there is still one thing hanging in the air. It is nothing deadly, but I am not prepared to tell you about it yet."

I was almost crazy with suspense, but I knew Phil would tell me whatever was on his mind when he was finally prepared. And I needed to see Miss Jessie as quickly as possible to tell her that Knight's Gate was finally safe once more. That Boz would never again be bothered by anyone from Crawford's crime connection or the Noah Cartel. That as Philo once said, "Noah is no Morah," at Knight's Gate.

I found Miss Jessie in the kitchen talking to Maria. They were discussing how southern cuisine and Mexican cuisine could be combined to get the most pleasing results for the human palate. Miss Jesse stopped the conversation just long enough to thank Phil and me for saving her job. Then it was back to the discussion of food and the pleasure of eating. I knew Miss Jessie Crum was back in the land of the living and freedom.

Chapter 42

As all the facts had finally come to light, Phil and I decided, in all fairness, Cramp at least should know the whole truth. We invited Ralph to go out with us for an evening meal. The other three old buds were off to various places taking care of business pertaining to their own financial concerns. Cramp had become almost exclusively dedicated to the success of Knight's Gate—he, like Philo, considered the Gate his earthly home. He continued to treat me as his own flesh and blood, and I returned the same feelings to him.

As we were eating our food, Phil suddenly addressed Ralph with the statement, "Cap, this time it wasn't really the mob."

Without a pause in the conversation, Ralph quickly replied, "Little buddy, as usual you are right again." Then a look of wonderment came over Ralph's face. After several moments of thought and three or four blinks of his eyes, in an amazed stammer he said, "Philo, is it really you behind those hideous glasses and those snake eyes?"

Phil removed his glasses and the contact lenses from his eyes and then spoke to Ralph in the plaintive voice of Philo Peabody. "I'm not dead, and I wish all of you would treat me more as a human than a Smurf."

Then Cramp took several deep gulping breaths as he began to stammer. "But, but how? I saw you buried in the front yard. You were killed in a gas explosion! How are you alive and why do you look so much different? Am I drunk or am I having a stroke and imagining all of this? Please tell me what's going on."

As Ralph began to gain control of himself, Phil began to explain. "Ralph, I was never really Philo. I was a government agent working undercover to discover why old men were mysteriously dying in retirement homes across the nation. I was born with an ailment that caused me to begin to age prematurely. Because of that I was able to live among you and not be suspected of being a plant. After the first Noah affair, my agency—Country Freedom—believed I could go to France and attempt to stop the aging process. I did and it worked. Then when Billy was killed, the agency decided to reinstate me back at Knight's Gate to try to stop the killings all over again. Noah, or young Kobb, tried to kill me, Philo, in Chicago, but I had to kill the assassin in self-defense, and then I came here as Dr. Elliot. Please keep my secret for a while longer, and then everyone will be able to know. And, oh yes, Abby and I are not an act. We really do love each other. And my real name is Phil Phelps."

Tears came to Ralph's eyes as he reached for Phil's hand. "I've missed you so much over the last many months. You had become my little brother, and I so enjoyed trying to take care of you."

Then it was Phil's turn as he also spoke with tears in his eyes. "Ralph, would you be content to be Abby's and my father? Or perhaps grandfather to any children we might have? We are going to be an official family in the near future."

Then tears came to my eyes as I realized what he was saying. I had to suppose he meant we would be getting married in the not-too-distant future. The meal was not the time or place, but as soon as we were alone I intended to find out all he had in mind.

As we continued to eat, I noticed that Ralph appeared to be an entirely different man. He sat straighter and held his head higher. I had to suppose the return of Philo improved his desire for life once more.

After taking Ralph back to Knight's Gate, Phil, with an embarrassed look on his face, asked if we needed to go to his apartment and discuss some things. I assured him I absolutely desired to talk.

Before we even entered his door he began to apologize. "Ab', I'm sorry I stated my intentions to Ralph before I said them to you. First, will you marry me? Second, I no longer work for Country Freedom. With the cutbacks in Washington, the security unit Country Freedom has been discontinued. I'm hoping you will continue to employee me at Knight's Gate. Fact is, this may be our last night in this fancy apartment as in the future it will not be paid for with government funds. That was the part left hanging that I didn't tell you after Kobb was arrested."

As he continued I felt a vast weight lift from my shoulders. He was finally going to be mine with not much danger connected to our association. I believed that with Robert Kobb being sent away no one else from Noah would come forward ever again. Putting my finger to Phil's lips, I nodded my head and whispered. "*Philo*, from this day forward you will have a home, a wife, children if possible, and a vast business where you will be needed every day." Then I kissed him and raced him to the bedroom to enjoy our love nest a little more before we would both be thrown out on our backsides.

After a very satisfying time in each other's arms, and Phil seeming more involved than before, I asked him what had changed. After some silent thought he answered. "Ab', I am finally free from all the pressures exerted by Crawford and the Noah Cartel. We are both safe, you have a successful business, we have friends, and we are going to be a married couple with perhaps kids of our own. Everything appears to be perfect in my life, with nothing that needs immediate attention."

At that point I butted in and said, "Sorry big boy, hold on to that last statement. We are going to need to hire a new physical trainer, because I fired the old one."

"Why did you fire Hector?"

"While you were busy on this last assignment, it came to light that Mr. Hector Ross had been establishing a harem inside the walls at Knight's Gate. Three of our nice young ladies fell under his charm, and he promised marriage to all three. I found two of them close to physically fighting each other over his affection. Then the third one came forward to tell me the other two were trying to steal Hector from her. Thankfully no new arrivals are expected to cause the stench to be worse than it was. But he did threaten me by telling me he knew you were not a licensed doctor and he was going to get some of the old men to sue you for fraud. So you will have to face that before you are totally free from worry."

Then Phil just laughed. "Ab', what that young man doesn't know is that Blank foresaw the possibility of such a problem, so he put me on undercover police work to protect you and our old gentlemen. He will vouch that I was not here as a doctor but as a law enforcement official on police business. Really the only thing left hanging was I needed to tell Cramp the whole story as he really deserved to know all about Philo and us. Now I've done that, so I suppose everything is cleared away."

Then I once more stated, "Remember, we also need a new physical trainer."

"No problem; one of my fellow Country Freedom agents, Guy Griffin, is a trained physical trainer and also will need another job. And, as luck would have it, he does not live too far from here. And, oh yes, he will not be chasing the little girls as he is middle-aged and has a wife and five children, two of which are still living at home. Plus, his wife would not put up with any hanky-panky and she outweighs Guy by several pounds. I think he was joking, but he once said she was a former marine."

Then it was my turn to laugh as I replied, "I'm not a former marine, but I better not catch you chasing the little chickens around Knight's Gate as I can also be a tough old bird."

Then he grinned and made one more remark, "I still remember when you killed Carlo Santos with one karate blow to the neck. You can bet your sweet bottom I won't challenge that."

Then it was back to one more tiny bit of serious lovemaking before it was time to get back to the work of running Knight's Gate Retirement Home for Mature Gentlemen.

Chapter 43

Some time later, as all the excitement settled, Phil and I were having a morning coffee and reviewing all that had happened. We believed—at least hoped—that the saga of all the questionable deaths at Knight's Gate had been solved. However, in the not-too-distant future, we both thought it necessary to unmask Dr. Elliot to all of Knight's Gate and return him to his actual identity, Phil Phelps.

As we traded thoughts and ideas, a wide grin appeared on Phil's face. "Oh Ab', I believe the sad tale of Hector Ross has also ended. I don't believe there will ever be a lawsuit against you, Knight's Gate, or me, concerning his firing. When I told Detective Blank about the threat Hector made, he decided to do an investigation of his own. Making a long story short, Hector Ross is not even his legal name— his full name is Hector Ross Simmons. He has worked all over the nation, just as he admitted, but he did not tell you the whole story. In two of his past employments he impregnated a young lady, and then he married both of them. However, he never divorced one before he married the other. He is married to one in Chicago under the name H. R. Simmons, and the other, in Atlanta, as Hector R. Simmons. When he came here he had already secured papers under the name Hector Ross. The law is looking for him, even as we speak. He has disappeared for now but will probably resurface in some other city, at some other retirement home, and try the same ruse. We can only hope he is caught before he destroys another girl's life. And we can be thankful our young attendant and you stopped him here before he hurt three more young ladies. But now, my love, it's time for the two of us to make plans for our future. And no, I am not married and never have been. But shortly I hope to be able to state otherwise."

With that statement a new thought entered my mind. "Phil, you know a lot about me, but I would like to know more about you. I don't even know your parents' names. Are your parents living?"

Then a strange look appeared in his eyes. "They're both dead, for many years. Actually, I barely remember them. And I remember my mother more than I remember my father. They were both killed in an automobile accident before I was five years old. I was raised in a church-sponsored orphanage. When I became of age to leave the orphanage I was moved into a high school sponsored by the same church. One of the preachers from the church and his wife allowed me to live with them until I graduated high school, and then I entered the military. I did not like living with them because they wanted me to become a preacher, and I did not believe I was meant to be a minister. In the army I was assigned to intelligence work and trained in hand-to-hand combat. I became very proficient in both disciplines. At about the time I entered the military, my premature aging began. After a few years the U.S. government secured my release from the army and moved me into a branch of Homeland Security, into their intelligence division. With a little makeup I could be middle-aged, and without makeup I could play the part of an old man. That's how I ended up at Knight's Gate. You pretty well know the rest, and that is also the reason I didn't know much about women when we first met."

With a quick kiss, I whispered in his ear, "That's why I'm so happy I caught you when I did."

Then he said, "Their names were Phillip and Ella Mae, and they're buried in Alton, Illinois.

Chapter 44

One morning as things at Knight's Gate seemed to have almost totally settled down, one of the attendants came to me to ask a favor. Not a favor for himself, but one coming from Dan. "Ms. Jordan, Mr. Herdon asked me to tell you he needs a big favor. And it is a favor of the utmost importance, concerning his estate. He asked that you come immediately as his time is not guaranteed and he needs to get something taken care of before he goes."

With a lot of questions going through my mind, I went immediately to Dan's room. When I arrived, Dan seemed to be in a better-than-usual state and was actually smiling as I walked in. "Dan, what is all the rush about? You appear to be ready to stay with us for quite a while."

In his slow, low, halting speech, Dan explained his desires. "Miss Abby, I have a few things I need to get done with my estate before I die. I've been studying on it for several days, and I believe I have things thought out as to what I want to do with my estate. First, do you think Mr. Smiley would make out a will for me? I understand he is a lawyer and former judge. I have some money put away, and I do not want the government to get it when I'm gone. Miss Abby, it is dirty money. It came from my work with the cartel. It has been the Devil's stash for many years, and now I want it to do good for someone who deserves it."

"Dan, I'm sure Leo would be pleased to help you clear your mind and see that your money goes wherever you wish it to go. And you are in luck as he is in town for a few days helping Knight's Gate clear up all the details stemming from Billy's death and Robert's arrest. I'll contact him immediately and try to get him here, even today if possible."

"Oh yes, also, Miss Abby, could you, Dr. Elliot, and Cramp be witnesses to my last testament. I'm sure there are others from the cartel who would like to claim my money for themselves. But with three witnesses I believe they would have no way of breaking my will."

"Whatever it takes, we will be sure it is done right and lawful. Leo Smiley is one smart lawyer and a great friend of Knight's Gate."

Dan seemed satisfied with the plan, so I hurried back to my office to attempt to make an appointment with Leo. Finding him still in his rooms on campus, I asked the favor, and he agreed to do the task as soon as possible.

Then, of course, it was back to the office and the hated paperwork before lunch. *Oh well,* I thought, *perhaps Miss Jessie will prepare my favorite soup, and that will make me feel a whole lot better.*

Chapter 45

Luck was with Dan, and Leo was able to see him the middle of the same afternoon. Phil and I were free at the time, and Ralph said he seldom had anything to do, so he was also available. We decided we would move Dan's bed out of his room and wheel it into one of the larger empty rooms that had a table and some chairs.

When Leo arrived, the rest of us assembled in the chosen room. I asked Dan if there were any papers or other physical information he might have that would be needed for the meeting. He assured me that all the information we needed was in his head.

Leo opened his briefcase and started pulling out forms and loose pages he would need to fulfill Dan's request for a will. First, he had Dan state his full name, age, birth date, and many other pertinent facts confirming Dan's true identity. Second, Dan was required to identify any holdings or property he claimed title to.

Dan explained that all of his holdings were in the form of cash money or cash paying investments, and that they were dispersed in various banks and holding companies, both in the U.S. and some foreign countries. Then he told Leo the amount of the total holdings was in the neighborhood of three million dollars, or perhaps more.

Leo handed Dan a form and told him to write the names of the holding companies and their locations. This took Dan a while as he was forced to stop and rest several times. After Dan completed this task, Leo asked Dan if he felt strong enough to write the deposit codes next to the holding companies' names. He had Dan write them so the rest of us would not have access to the codes.

Then Leo suggested we take a break for coffee and snacks so Dan could nap a little before we continued. Everyone was ready except Dan. He stopped us and made one more statement. "If I should die during this break, everything goes to Miss Jessie. Then he closed his eyes, and we heard a slight snoring.

After an hour or so of visiting and discussing the current happenings at the Gate, an attendant came and told us Dan was once more awake, alert, and appearing to want to continue with the meeting. Leo had already reviewed the information Dan had given him and was moving on to the distribution of his estate. We had all wondered about his last statement before his nap and felt we would now get the facts as to Miss Jessie being his heir.

Leo's first question was, "Now Dan, how do you want your estate to be distributed?"

Dan, in a little more than a whisper, declared, "As I told you before the break, whatever I have left when I leave this world, I want to go to Miss Jessie."

"You are saying Miss Jessie Crum is to be your beneficiary?" Leo asked.

"Yes. I was sent here to spy on that lady and then learned her only concern was for us old men. After I was finally free from all cartel activities, I decided I wanted her to have a good life if I could swing it. And now it looks like I'll be able to. I took the job with the cartel because I wanted to. Miss Jessie was forced into what she did because she had to. Now I hope I've evened the score."

"She is to be your only heir?"

"Yes."

"Dan, I'm sure I can get it done."

"Oh yes, you are to take your fees out of the funds before the balance goes to Miss Jessie."

"Dan, this work will be pro bono, as you are now one of the family members at Knight's Gate and I do not take payment from my family members."

"Mr. Leo, I'm so proud to have a brother like you." As Dan handed the papers back to Leo after signing the will, we once more heard the light snoring. Then it was Phil's, Cramp's, and my turn to sign our names as witnesses to Dan Herdon's will.

As Phil and I left the room, hand in hand, I felt a sense of light around me. Perhaps Billy's death did mean something, as I had also just witnessed a flash of goodness out of all the darkness.

Chapter 46

Slowly, oh so slowly, life at Knight's Gate settled into everyday humdrum, and Phil and I started to make plans for our future. Unlike other couples our age, finance was not an issue. The business was carrying its own weight, and with my father's estate and the money the old buds were spending, as they cared to, around the place, life was delightful.

One morning as I began my day, checking details of residents, staff, and supplies, Phil told me I had an appointment with one of the ladies' shops in Galeton. I did not understand, but he said it was very important to his and my future in the operation of the Gate. He assured me he could handle anything that might arise in the office. Cramp was present at that moment and supported Phil with the statement, "What he can't handle, I can." With that type of assurance, I considered I would love an hour or so away from work, and a ladies' shop was just too much temptation. Quickly taking a few dollars out of my personal stash and grabbing my checkbook, I was on my way.

The Queen's Shoppe was considered the only place a lady of means would ever frequent for the best line of apparel. What business Phil had drummed up with one of the best garment businesses in the area, I couldn't fathom. I thought perhaps one of the owners or an associate was looking for a spot for an older male relative, and we would be honored as the retirement home of their choice. As I entered the door of the shop, I was immediately surrounded by the main manager and two other assistants. The manager took my hand as she made me welcome.

"Ms. Jordan, it's such a pleasure for the Queen's Shoppe to be chosen to dress you and your attendants for your upcoming ceremony. Your fiancé and his father have assured me that we were your choice alone to fulfill all the requirements of such a gala event. Let me be the first to congratulate you and beg for your indulgence as we fit you with one of our finest wedding gowns."

I knew I was a gutsy woman, but I almost fainted as she completed her statement. Suddenly I was the happiest woman alive, and at the same time I wanted to strangle Phil and Cramp, as I knew they were having a hilarious time at my expense. Quickly I regained control of my emotions and fell right into the swing of the event. It was as if I was the only woman in the shop as all the attendants gathered around me at once. Then I saw...I *was* the only woman in the shop. Someone had closed the display window blinds, and one of the attendants was locking the door. The manager smiled and explained that the shop was being paid by a Mr. Leo Smiley to be closed for a couple of hours to accommodate his granddaughter as she was being dressed for her wedding.

So...the whole stinking crowd is involved in this farce, I thought. But God how I loved the whole stinking crowd.

In a few minutes, six of the most beautiful wedding dresses I had ever seen were placed in front of me to choose from. For my first wedding, if my memory was correct, I was wearing a cheap suit off a rack and a veil off another rack. This time I was going to be a true bride with the complete trousseau.

"Oh yes, Ms. Jordan, your uncle, Sandy Gallman, also congratulates you by agreeing to purchase your dress for the occasion." I felt tears in my eyes.

In a short time I was fitted with a long, slim, shift-cut gown of white satin with half sleeves and a low-cut back. The veil slightly covered my face but fell to the waist in the back. The shoes were soft satin footsies just covering my feet. Undergarments, no comment.

In about an hour my wedding dress and accessories were chosen and prepared for alterations, where needed. The things needing no alterations I carried out in boxes and bags. I thanked the manager and staff as I left the shop and headed to my car. I grinned as I thought to myself, *Abby, it appears you are about to become a bride.* I certainly hoped the gang had Phil in mind to be the groom.

Chapter 47

When I exited my car at the front door of Knight's Gate, a contingency of friends and interested parties were waiting. Phil immediately stepped forward accompanied by John "Sparky" Niles, the third of the old buds. As I moved closer to Phil he promptly assumed a kneeling position as Sparky handed him a small object over his shoulder from behind. Taking the small object in his right hand he cleared his throat and addressed me in a very formal manner. "Ms. Jordan, it has come to my attention that you have been waiting patiently for almost two years for a true token of my affection. Mr. Niles decided the only thing that would fulfill the place of such a token had to be an engagement ring. I agreed with Mr. Niles's conclusion, so he is giving you such a ring. And, if your answer to my next question is in the affirmative, I will also supply a wedding ring to match. Ms. Jordan, will you accept me, Philo Peabody, Phil Phelps, as an acceptable candidate to become your husband?"

Pretending to ignore him as I started to pass him by, I replied so all could hear. "Only if my four elder relatives feel that you are a satisfactory match for such an illustrious bride. You understand a princess can only marry a commoner with the consent of the king and older princes."

From four elder mouths and many more in the crowd I heard a loud reply. "Yes, Yes, Yes. Philo the Smurf definitely needs a keeper in his life."

With that reply I stood still long enough for Phil to slip the ring on my finger. I knew it would fit because Phil always did his homework. Then I grabbed him and kissed him as if I would never let him go. And I intended to truly never let him go.

Later as I gathered more of the packages from the car, Miss Jessie stopped me in the hall and said, "Miss Abby, Maria and I are planning a wedding dinner like none ever seen in Galeton. We are so happy for you and Mr. Phil. And I know you are going to have a nice family of your own in a few years. That's another thing my Granny gave me. I have the gift to see things like that before they happen."

I put the packages down and placed my arms around that woman and hugged until I was afraid I might hurt her. But she squeezed me just as tightly and whispered, "Miss Abby, I love you like a sister."

I placed my lips close to her ear and replied, "I never had a sister, but God could never have given me one that I could have loved more than you."

When I next saw Dan Herdon, he struggled to reach my hand as he labored to tell me, "Ms. Jordan," then there was a pause, "I'm so sorry," another pause, "I was ever involved in Noah." And then after many pauses he finally completed his thought. "I was probably involved in your father's death, and for that I'm so sorry. But I will never be sorry for knowing you." Then he closed his eyes, and I heard him begin to snore.

As the days passed, I finally fully realized that Phil and Cramp had been passing the story around about Phil's background so no one would ever wonder how the events of the Noah Cartel took place at Knight's Gate.

But, even though every one of our staff had been around when Billy was poisoned, it appeared they wanted to let it go and fade away. They all simply did their jobs, collected their salaries, and continued to live their lives in the way they wanted and were accustomed to. The approaching wedding and the anticipated celebration seemed to fulfill all the needs they had. And I began to be filled with anticipation also. Perhaps that is the way it should be—forget the past sorrow, live in the present, and enjoy the anticipation.

Chapter 48

Without my knowledge Phil had been busy making all the arrangements for our wedding. I was certain however, he had a lot of assistance from Cramp and the other three old buds. His reasoning for a rushed wedding date, or so he explained, was our ages and our desire for children. He said he believed every day we waited was a day counted against us. I said I believed Miss Jessie when she said we would have a family.

Then he said, "Abby, I hope you will not be mad, but I have made plans for our wedding to take place in two weeks."

I started to feel a bit taken advantage of but then thought for a moment and decided, "Why not?" I wanted to marry the man, so what did it matter if it was sooner rather than later? From that moment on I was all-in. After realizing how hard he was working to get us married, I decided I could be of help by doing some of the planning myself.

Phil, at the time not being a church person, left it up to me to secure a minister and a musician. I did not believe securing a minister would be that tough a job. I remembered the little man who did Philo's burial, and he still lived at Knight's Gate. All I had to do was ask him.

The older gentleman who had spoken at Philo's funeral agreed to also preside at Phil's and my wedding. Reverend Limkohler was a somewhat rotund little man of German descent, with a deep love of God and a fantastic sense of humor. His home had been a little farming community in mid-Missouri, and he later had become a resident of Knight's Gate because his daughter lived in East St. Louis, Illinois.

Displaying a huge grin, he said with a slight German brogue, "In all my years as a reverend, this is the only time for me to be the minister at a man's burial one day and within a few months conduct his marriage ceremony." Then he gave forth a deep belly laugh. As I had believed, the old gentleman was delighted to be asked to do the Lord's work once again.

Finding a musician was a completely different story. I tried everywhere with no results. I finally decided I would just have to hire a pianist from one of the unions in St. Louis or Chicago. It would be a bit of a drive from either city, but if he or she was a paid professional, they would make the trip.

Chapter 49

The big day finally arrived, and with it, all the usual stomach butterflies and pounding in the head. I was convinced that everything would be perfect with Phil in charge, but deep in my being I was still afraid he would miss something. All I could do was hope for the best as Rose Mary and I dressed for the ceremony.

One of the exercise gyms at Knight's Gate had been cleared of all the workout equipment and had been redecorated as a small chapel. From outside the double-door entry it looked the same as it had always looked, but once inside it looked like a chapel in a small church. A small podium had been constructed and carpeted, with an American walnut lectern at center front. Fake stained-glass windows had been attached to the walls. A baby grand piano was placed in one front corner. Folding chairs were available, stacked against the back wall. Everything in the room, save the piano, chairs, and lectern was painted snow white, and there were fresh cut flowers everywhere. There was not much room for seating, but we believed the attendance would be less than fifty, and more like thirty. But, the old buds spared no expense to assure every detail was correct. Their daughter was going to be married in the finest of style.

My mind wandered back over the past week as I reran all the arrangements through my mind one more time. Cramp, being the oldest by just a few months, would have the honor of giving the bride away. He would give me away in the name of my father, Robert Carew, and my mother, Magdalene Jordan.

I had been taken totally by surprise when Rose Mary Smith asked me if I had a maid of honor. And, oddly enough, I really did not have anyone in mind. With her head down almost in a bow, she asked, "Ms. Jordan, I know this is not the way it works, but would you allow me to be your maid of honor? My father treated you so badly.

133

Yes, now I know the whole story about him wanting you killed. And, even after that, you and Dr. Elliot...I mean Mr. Phelps...have treated me so well, I feel I owe a debt I can never repay. So, I would deem it a great honor to serve you in your wedding, and at the same time would feel you have forgiven me for all the things my father did."

Without a moment of hesitation I said, "Nurse Smith, would you do me the honor of being my maid of honor in my wedding to Mr. Phil Phelps on the coming Sunday afternoon?"

"Oh yes, and thank you so much. Miss Abby, I really love you for being who you are." Then she continued, "I believe you have been looking for a pianist for the ceremony. My little sister would play for you if I asked her."

I was so happy, the only reply I could muster was, "Please!" Then I directed her to take her sister and go to the Queen's Shoppe to be fitted with the proper dresses for the occasion.

I had also visited Dan and asked him if we moved his bed to the door of the little chapel, would he agree to attend my wedding?

With a smile on his face, he replied in his halting, breathing way, "Ms. Jordan, if the bastards don't get me or if God or the Devil does not call for me, I would deem it my greatest honor to see you being wed." Then the soft snoring began again.

Alma, my duplex mate, and Brad Blank also planned to attend. The only one who would miss the ceremony was the old Philo. But, I was still happy as Phil would substitute very well.

Chapter 50

I could hear the piano being played softly as Rose Mary and I arrived from my duplex, where we had gone to dress. One of the young male attendants picked us up and drove us back to Knight's Gate.

As we arrived out front of the home, another surprise was waiting—a red carpet had been rolled out, leading into the front door of the Gate. Two of the young attendants dressed in blue tuxedos escorted Rose Mary and me inside the front doors and to the make-believe chapel doors. At that point Rose Mary proceeded toward the altar, and Ralph stepped in beside me as we waited for the wedding march to commence. Cramp was dressed in a blue tux with a bright-red tie as an accessory.

As I looked through the glass of the double doors, I saw that the entire male wedding party was attired in blue tuxedos with red ties. The scheme—with the white of the chapel—was red, white, and blue. Phil was extremely patriotic and had worked undercover for the welfare of our nation and her citizens. I felt a rush of pride for the man I was about to wed.

Then I heard the piano sound the first bars of the wedding march as Ralph and I entered the doors and solemnly marched toward the altar, where my love was waiting. After repeating our simple and honest vows and exchanging rings, Reverend Limkohler pronounced us man and wife in the eyes of God and our peers.

As Phil raised my veil and moved toward me for our wedding kiss, he quickly whispered to me in the plaintive voice of Philo, "Ain't no Noah, no morah; just two Smurfs got hitched." After we kissed, Phil faced all our friends and announced, "Miss Jessie's team is waiting in the dining room with the wedding banquet!"

Almost everyone in attendance yelled "HURRAH!" and headed for the doors. However, they did wait for Phil and me to arrive before they attacked the food layout.

As we entered the dining room there was one more huge surprise—in the center of the room, on a round table, stood a five-foot-high, five-tiered wedding cake. On the top tier were the bride and groom dolls and the names Abby and Phil. On the next layer down was the name Ralph Cramp, the next Leo Smiley, then Sandy Gallman, and last John Niles—all the old bunch who began the fight against the Noah Cartel and was now a complete family. Tears came to my eyes and warmth to my heart. I squeezed Phil's hand a little tighter.

Miss Jessie and Maria totally out-cooked themselves. I remember beef, pork, and turkey as the major meat dishes. There may have been other meats, I just can't recall. Salads, more than six—both American and Mexican dishes. There were also finger foods of all types, with sauces and salsas for dipping. Wedding cake and hand-blended ice cream finished the layout. To drink, there was coffee, American and Mexican tea, soft drinks, and I'm afraid some of the young people brought in liquor. The lighter variety, I hoped.

A couple of hours, pounds, and inches later, most of the guests had left the dining area looking for someplace to nap or allow time to digest their rewards.

Phil, Cramp, Gallman, Smiley, Niles, and I slipped away to one of the vacant rooms and sampled a very expensive bottle of champagne that was delivered by an old friend of Phil's from the Peabody Foundation, aka Country Freedom. Country Freedom was no longer a government agency, but it still existed behind closed doors and was financed by several very wealthy patriotic citizens of the nation. I was a little worried that Phil would want to continue being an agent for the organization, but he assured me all he wanted, going forward, was to be a happy husband and an ecstatic father if it was to be.

As I suspected, the champagne may have been expensive, but it still did not taste that good to me. I supposed I would just never be a drinker.

Chapter 51

After the wedding banquet Phil and I spent a day or two at my duplex. We were definitely going to have a honeymoon, we had just not ironed out all the plans involved—where we intended to go and for how long. We also could not decide if we wanted to drive somewhere or fly and rent a vehicle to see the area.

Ralph listened to our discussions for a while, and always with a grin on his face. It was as if he knew a secret and was bursting to divulge it to someone else. Finally he could contain himself no longer. Cramp had decided to keep his wedding gift a secret until after the wedding ceremony. He finally presented to Phil and me a new state-of-the-art, self-contained camping vehicle, along with several gift cards to buy fuel on the road. He explained we were to take a long leisurely honeymoon and see some or all the American continent. He further explained he had been in negotiations with a firm that specialized in the business operations of various types of companies, and while we were traveling he wanted to see if they could run a business such as Knight's Gate. He said he would remain in total command until they proved they could, or could not, handle the daily routine of operating a retirement home. And, when we returned, perhaps we would no longer be forced to run the retirement home on a day-to-day basis. We could be on a permanent honeymoon all the time and still have a solid business making us a living.

We decided to give it a try, and we began to pack the unit with everything necessary to sustain us for at least a month. In that time we felt we would discover whether we could enjoy the open road or not.

Phil, in his job before he went undercover, had traveled a lot in the east, so we discussed seeing the western side of the U.S. Since I had never traveled much farther than Chicago and St. Louis, the west sounded as exciting as any other place in the nation. So, it was decided our first attempt at living the good life would be in the desert southwest, the California coast, and the northwest with its rugged ocean front and big trees. I became so excited I could hardly contain myself. I was thrilled to be able to spend the time with the love of my life.

The day finally arrived, and we set sail for the area where the sun goes to sleep. As we exited the parking lot of Knight's Gate, I realized my real life had begun there and would probably someday end there. When I had experienced all that life offered, I believed I would be totally satisfied.

***

Now, as I sit here at my computer, having ended the tale of murder at Knight's Gate Retirement Home for Mature Gentlemen, I've permitted myself to relive and rethink the past eighteen months of my life. During those months I have been allowed, by fate, to become almost a complete woman.

During that time, my happiest reward was meeting the man of my dreams. My grandest reward was being able to know my mother and meet my father before his untimely death in a murder-for-hire and money-laundering scheme. My ultimate reward would be to have a child or children of my own.

I was also allowed to meet and be informally adopted by four old gentlemen who lived at Knight's Gate. They were, after my husband, the loves of my life. The only greater love would be for children of my own.

Also during that time I became a highly successful businesswoman. Running Knight's Gate was a challenge but also gave me much pleasure as the four old buds and I have watched it expand and improve.

To make this tale complete, you need to be informed that Billy Ashfort's family was awarded an insurance liability claim of 3.75 million dollars in their wrongful death suit. Money can never replace the life of a loved one lost, but if the family uses the money wisely, they should never want for anything the rest of their lives.

Now it is time for me to return to my job as owner/operator of Knight's Gate. But I would like to leave you with the following wishes from two of my favorite staff members. From Miss Jessie Crum: "May the good Lord love and keep you," and from her assistant, Miss Maria Elena Aguilar: "Vaya con Dios, amigos!"

I hope this story brought you some enjoyment and perhaps a smile or a tear.

Abigail Jordan Carew Devine Phelps

Abigail Jordan Carew Devine Phelps

EPILOGUE

A few years have passed since the last murder at Knight's Gate Retirement Home for Mature Gentlemen. Now the older residents look forward to spending their final years in one of the nation's finest retirement centers. Phil and I—Phil Phelps and Abigail Jordan Carew Devine Phelps—have been married long enough to be the proud parents of first a fine young son, Ralph Robert Phelps, the Godson of Ralph Cramp and future owner of Cramp's used car empire. Then second, a beautiful daughter, Ella Abigail Phelps, named for Phil's mother and me, and heiress to the estate of Robert Carew, her grandfather.

Knight's Gate is now operated by a professional nursing-home firm, as I and the four old buds live the good life as overseers of the business without the daily headaches of paperwork and details. Phil does consultations on security and personal self-defense for self-employed businessmen. Our family lives in a nice, but not extravagant, home in Galeton, Illinois. I kept my apartment, and it is used to house visiting dignitaries and long-term visiting relatives of old men living at the Gate.

Dan Herdon, finally, could no longer beat the bastards of death and is honorably buried in the garden at Knight's Gate.

Ralph Cramp is totally retired from his business empire, and it is being run by a banking and business firm until his death, and then it will be the property of Ralph Robert Phelps. Cramp still lives in his private quarters at Knight's Gate and also desires to be entombed in the home's garden.

The other three old buds have almost entirely returned to their own business empires. All three still have their own private rooms at the Gate, but they seldom appear on-site. Someday I'm sure ownership of their private quarters will be returned to Knight's

Gate. At present, with the permission of the owners, the rooms are used as overflow for visiting dignitaries.

After Dan Herdon's death, Miss Jessie inherited his estate of approximately four million dollars. Almost immediately she took an early retirement from Knight's Gate and moved to Chicago. Her son Bozworth Crum was released from prison, and he and his mother opened a halfway house in a building the City of Chicago gave them. The location is in an area of homes belonging to those of lesser income. Miss Jessie operates the kitchen and feeds the residents, while Boz handles the cleaning and upkeep. They named the station, "The Jessie Boz House."

Maria Aguilar assumed the head chef position at the Gate and is slowly making her reputation as a fine cook in hopes of approaching a level of competence comparable to that of Miss Jessie Crum.

Bradley Blank is now chief of detectives for the city of Galeton's police department and still uses the inheritance from his grandfather, Sal Calone, to help those less fortunate.

Phil's friend, Guy Griffin, became the new physical trainer at the Gate, replacing Hector Ross. He has made himself a successful career.

Hector Ross made one more run at a young lady in Philadelphia and was shot and killed by her gang-related boyfriend, a sad but ultimate fate.

Philo's grave is kept up well in the beautiful gardens of Knight's Gate. For most, the truth of his existence is still kept secret. We who know the truth simply smile when he is mentioned. But, for others, he is a symbol of a creature that was made incorrectly but was allowed to live his own life with a warm place to call home and friends who loved him. May all men, and women, of his ilk be afforded, at least, a like lifestyle.

About the Author

Roger Baker retired from teaching school after twenty-nine years of service.

During his career in education, he used storytelling as a means to enrich his classroom presentations and capture the attention of his students.

He has been spending leisure hours of his retirement with storytelling, now with his pen. He and his wife reside in central Missouri.

Roger has published two other novels, *Two for the Price*, and *The Reverend and the Peacemaker*. This is the sequel to *Two for the Price*.

www.ingramcontent.com/pod-product-compliance
Lightning Source LLC
Chambersburg PA
CBHW071527170626
46811CB00007B/2969